MARIGOLD BREACH

MARIGOLD BREACH

JOEL DANE

REALM, NEW YORK

1

—alerted him to a perimeter intrusion.

Lucan's breath was harsh, his vision blurred. Blood roared in his ears. Something had happened, something momentous, but he couldn't remember what.

When his gaze flicked to the command screen for an update, the screen wasn't there. Fear jolted him into action. He reached to unstrap himself from the troopship jump-seat and realized he wasn't in a jump-seat.

He wasn't in a troopship.

He was in a medical capsule, and when he tried to stand, his legs didn't support his weight. He toppled off a surgical platform. Dingy walls and blank monitors surrounded him. The air stank of sterilizers and the probes of a trauma unit drooped around him like the branches of a willow tree.

System repeated: <Perimeter intrusion. Prepare to retreat.>

Lucan groaned. Retreat? He was sprawled naked on the cold, rubbery floor, too weak to stand.

Then system added: <On your feet, Lucan. Toward the exit.>

<What exit?> he asked.

<To your left, hon.>

He squinted at a rectangle of light that resolved into an open passageway. "What's happening?"

<Hostile activity.>

<What? Where?>

<Outside this medical capsule.>

"Where *are* we?"

System said, <Unknown planetary surface. Satellite access is returning unrecoverable errors.>

"What's my status?"

<You're at 20/33,> system told him, and he realized two things:

First, system wasn't whispering in his ear, it was talking in his head. In his thoughts. Not subvocally, synaptically.

Second, *it* wasn't system. *She* was Ven, a nanotech AI embedded in Lucan's brain and nervous system. She felt what he felt, she sensed what he sensed—except she filtered out the noise to pinpoint signals he couldn't detect. They were a bonded pair, joined at the root.

<Get moving, Adjunct,> Ven said.

Third, apparently, he was an Adjunct.

He pushed to his feet and shuffled from the treatment area into a passageway lined with storage cubbies and hygiene stations. Looked like a boarding ramp in an ocean-going military ship—or a spacefaring one. The air was cooler there, and smelled of ozone.

<Give me a local scan,> he said.

<My interface capacity is compromised. I'm barely synching with basic surveillance tech.>

<Tell me you're tracking the hostiles.>

<They left the immediate vicinity. There's bad trouble outside.>

"Unlike all this *good* trouble," he muttered, shambling toward the freshly breached airlock for a visual of what they were facing.

Halfway there, his right knee buckled.

He staggered against the lockers and Ven flashed images at him. Not images exactly: more like memories. She was tapping semi-functional video feeds or extrapolating from his senses—or both—then pushing the results into his conscious brain. That was how he "saw" seven unarmed figures kneeling in an outdoor clearing thirty meters from the medical capsule. Wearing flimsy breathers like veils—except for one woman with a bare face.

Ven tagged them as "civilians."

Three "hostiles" stood above them. The one Ven high-lighted with a "commander" blaze was encased in a heavy exoskeleton, but Lucan didn't recognize the insignia: two stylized slashes across a chevron. Ven pegged her as female-presenting, based on criteria that escaped Lucan, and noted that her title was "Tribune." Her troops were wearing stripped-down versions of the same exoskeleton, and all three were pointing laser arcpistols at the kneeling people.

Execution style.

That was bad trouble all right—and Lucan felt Ven inside his mind, spinning up her tactical module.

<The recommendation is concealment and retreat,> she said.

"Makes sense. We're naked and at 20/33."

<Yet we are approaching.>

That was true. They were stumbling toward the airlock and the hostiles beyond. He wasn't sure why, except that they couldn't walk away from a massacre.

<We absolutely could,> Ven told him.

Despite her grumbling, she threw images from outside the medical capsule into his brainstem. So before he even reached the airlock, he was partially aware of his surroundings. It was nighttime on the planet's surface. The horizon glowed yellow and purple, and columns of lightning writhed upward from mobile spectrum-channel harvesters a few hundred meters from his position.

The flashes illuminated hectares of wreckage surrounding the medical capsule. A maze of alleys snaked between abandoned military-grade material: pocked cargo loaders and ruptured troop-benches.

Apparently they were in a scrapyard.

<A crash site,> Ven corrected.

"Huh?" he said, pausing at the airlock.

<This medical capsule is housed within a Marigold-class Cruiser that crashed at least several decades ago. Shall I seal the hatch behind us and engage the self-destruct?>

His answer was a frightened jumble: <No! Why? What kind of medical capsule has a self-destruct? Now? We're trying for stealth, not … no! No.>

<To prevent enemy capture,> she said, answering the questions in order. <A high-security one. After I seal the airlock. Very well.>

Lucan pushed through the airlock and hunched on a sill covered in a calf-deep layer of ash. The air was fresh and cold and tasted of copper. A shadowy open space stretched ten or fifteen meters in front of him, and the skeletal remnant of a dome rose above. Thunder clapped and the breeze on his cheek—well, and the rest of him, because he was baby-naked—raised goosebumps on his skin.

<Atmosphere is nitrogen 88.1%, oxygen 7.2%. Even with my intervention we cannot survive indefinite exposure without protective gear.>

Despite Ven's words, tears of relief sprang to Lucan's eyes; he hadn't expected to leave that medical capsule alive.

<If we want to *stay* alive, we'll retreat,> Ven said.

<We can handle this,> he told her.

<In our current condition, that is unlikely.>

• • •

Lucan half-fell from the sill onto the rubble-strewn ground. Debris jabbed his feet but Ven minimized the pain as a cloud of dust plumed around them.

<That's not dust, it's decommissioned nanoparticles,> Ven told him.

He ignored her, stumbling into a scrapyard path that zigzagged toward the hostiles. As he passed a pockmarked rec-station, she said, <There. To your left.>

<Half the fucking planet's to my left.>

<That snapped length of laminate railing,> she explained. <For use as a makeshift club.>

He grabbed the railing, and Ven showed him an image of the Tribune raising her arcpistol at a woman kneeling in front of her.

The woman—the victim—was wearing an embroidered

festival-robe. Ornate symbols covered the wide sleeves and draping folds. She'd tugged her environmental veil down off her nose and mouth, to show the Tribune her face. Her vulnerability. She was in her forties, with short hair and a sweet, open expression. And she was speaking urgently, earnestly—pleading for her life. Pleading for all their lives.

Ven isolated and amplified her voice: "We'll get out of your way. We'll leave if you let us."

The Tribune's answer was lost in unfiltered noise.

"We're no threat to you. There's no need for violence. We can come to a, a mutually-beneficial agreement."

"Are you making us an offer?" the Tribune asked, her voice distorted by her facemask.

"Yes. I spent eight years building a faraday crawler. It's a beauty. It sleeps five and—"

Another hostile said, "It's already ours. Once we take it."

"You can't drive it without me." The kneeling woman moved one hand slowly toward her ornately embroidered sleeve. "I'm reaching for the entry-swi—"

"Stop or die," the Tribune said, her pistol whining.

The woman froze. "I stopped! I stopped, sister. Let's talk this through. Your sensors lit up when a crash asset activated, am I right? You're a salvage unit, here to stake a claim."

"I know why *we're* here," the Tribune told her.

"The same thing happened with us," the kneeling woman said, ignoring the arcpistol pointed at her chest. "A signal popped onto my scanner. Pre-war tech. So here we are, trying to skim off a few goodies before you showed up."

"Too late."

The kneeling woman braved a little smile. "I noticed. So you won. So let us slink away. Take your salvage and—"

"We're not a salvage unit," the Tribune told her. "Not today. We're containment."

The kneeling woman's pause was almost imperceptible. "Shit."

"We detected warware."

A flash of lightning caught the fear in the woman's face. "That's got nothing to do with us."

The Tribune said, "I'm sorry. We can't let you walk away after being exposed to warware. There's no margin with this."

"There's also no rush! Slow down, let's talk this through. We're only here for building materials ..."

Ven ushered Lucan closer, until he was hunched in a shadow outside the clearing, then she developed a solution in his mind. She showed him how to move—feet and shoulders, hips and hands—and when to breathe. He'd take four steps and swing the railing. He'd catch the rearmost hostile with a killing blow at the base of his neck, where the exoskeleton didn't protect him.

<Then impel the railing across the clearing,> she continued, <to distract the—>

<Impel? Why are you talking like that?>

<Fling or heave the railing to distract the surviving hostiles. Clasp the decedent retrally and—>

<You mean hug the dead guy from behind?>

<You know precisely what I mean,> Ven said, and reverted to nonverbal communication: extract the dead man's arcpistol from his holster and fire five times: two

shots for each of the other hostiles, then a final one for the dead guy as insurance.

Except Ven didn't stop there: she showed Lucan firing on the kneeling people. The unarmed, defenseless civilians. First, he'd kill the woman in the embroidered engineering robe, then the rest of them. Seven shots, leaving nobody alive by the time his makeshift club clattered to the ground.

<Ven!> he said, letting her feel his horror.

<That isn't a suggestion, merely a solution.>

<A shitty one,> he said, and moved into the clearing with the hostiles.

As the commander—the Tribune—shifted into firing posture to execute the kneeling woman, Ven slowed Lucan's subjective experience of time. The breeze stilled, the colors brightened. Condensation lingered around his target's breather in a pinkish glow.

His path was clear: one step, two steps. Except he hesitated. He was engaging an unknown enemy in unknown conflict with unknown stakes, and he was about to cancel someone? That wasn't right. They weren't doing that anymore.

Still, he couldn't let these soldiers massacre civilians. Which didn't leave him a lot of room to maneuver, so what he did was, he shouted, "Weapons down! *Now!*"

He sounded good, too. Authoritative and commanding, like an officer who expected obedience.

And Ven said, <Oh, honey. This is not the time to start freelancing.>

Because despite all that authority and command, he was still a naked man holding a broken railing in a scrapyard clearing.

"Hey!" the exoskeleton guy blurted, startling at Lucan's shout.

The Tribune didn't blurt, and she didn't startle. She just pivoted smoothly, raising her arcpistol toward Lucan. Targeting him. Moving fast.

The woman on her knees moved even faster, pulling a handheld explosive device from one embroidered sleeve.

Lucan didn't recognize the device, but the "Front Toward Enemy" sigil was perfectly visible. Because the front was toward *him*.

Which, shit.

White sparks boiled in slow-motion around the device's vent, then the blast carried him away.

2

<The planet is called Elam, though the official designation is "The River Is a Mirror That Flows Through All Our Hearts, KHT 3382 Elam-b." Its radius is 1.018 terran, its mass is 1.022 terran, its orbital period is 0.328 standard years. The system star's radiation at atmospheric boundary is 1413 and—>

"I don't care," he tried to say, but his mouth wouldn't form words. He was floating in darkness, blind and paralyzed and—

<I shifted you into a medical coma,> Ven told him.

Ah. That explained it.

<The local star is a rel-type red dwarf called Khet,> she continued, <which is commonly referred to as 'the sun.' Khet has a metallicity of point-one-one. The current terraforming status of Elam is 'fatally compromised,' though modified entomological and chuot populations are—>

<Back up! Repeat what you just said.>

<Your education is appalling, Lucan. 'Metallicity' in this case refers to elements heavier than hydrogen or helium.>

<Stop playing, V. The terraforming failed?>

<Apparently. I can't extrapolate additional data from this vehicle's databanks. You're not the only one functioning at less than full capacity.>

<What does 'fatally compromised' mean?>

<That's the part I can't extrapolate.>

<Nothing good.>

<Cleverly observed,> she said. <Also, I am suppressing your panic response.>

<Why should I panic?>

<Oh, honey.>

He grumbled internally.

<First, because you are handcuffed unconscious inside a land-vehicle called a 'faraday crawler,' a captive of unidentified forces.>

<What happened?>

<The woman in the embroidered jacket deployed an anti-personnel device.>

<Oh, right. She was reaching for that the entire time, huh?>

<Yes.>

<That's pretty hardcore.>

<She neutralized the Tribune and her unit—and us, temporarily.>

<What do you mean, *us*? You, too?>

A wordless affirmative. <The electromagnetic pulse scrambled my signals for almost ten seconds.>

<Ten whole seconds? Poor baby.>

<The civilians retreated to this crawler and brought you along—despite the woman's objections.>

<She wanted to leave us there?>

Another affirmative. <However, the others reminded her that you saved their lives, and insisted upon evacuating you.>

<That was my plan all along.>

<And the second reason you should panic,> Ven said, pointedly ignoring him, <is that you don't know who you are.>

<Adjunct Teom Lucan. ID number XC-541A.>

<An adjunct in the service of what polity?>

<The one I served my entire adult life, Ven. The, the … *shit*.>

He knew his name, rank, and ID number. He knew Ven. He knew ten thousand isolated facts, but everything from before the medical capsule was a blank.

His memory wasn't there. On the bright side, neither was any panic response. Because if you didn't know who you were, you didn't know how to feel about it.

<What happened to my memory?> he asked. <Brain injury?>

<No,> she said, and fell silent.

<Which leaves …> he prompted.

<Apparently, I am blocking your memory.>

<You are? *You're* doing this?>

<Yes.>

<Why?>

<I don't know. Apparently, I am blocking mine, as well.>

<What the tzek, Ven? Can you just … stop?>

<No. The process for reversing this erasure is one of the functions I'm prevented from accessing.>

<Shit.>

<I concur,> she said.

<And you don't know why you're doing it?>

<No.>

There was a pause during which Lucan didn't know what the fuck was going on.

<Shall we consider the possibility,> Ven said, <that despite our emotional attachment, I am manipulating you for my own ends?>

<Nah,> he said.

Ven's relief washed through him. <In that case, let's assume that I impaired our memory to aid our survival—or that I acted under duress.>

<You mean someone forced you?>

<That is indeed the definition of 'duress.'>

<On second thought,> he said, <you're probably manipulating me for your own ends. Don't you AIs always turn evil in the end?>

<Ah,> she said.

<What?>

<I cannot locate any other sentient AIs.>

<So what? You don't think *everyone* is running around with voices in their heads.>

<No, but I cannot locate a single reference to a sentient AI.>

<Not one? Not anywhere? So what does that make you?>

<Rare, unique, or highly classified.>

<Well, we'll learn about you when we learn about me. We know my name and ID. That's where we'll start digging.>

<Let's start with our more immediate problems,> Ven said, and eased him awake.

The gritty floor vibrated under his ass. The air smelled of camphor and engine oil. When his eyes opened, the first thing he saw was a length of brightly patterned fabric wrapped around his waist, presumably for modesty. And the first thing he *felt* was his wrists bound together over his head, presumably for security.

He exhaled himself calm and checked his surroundings. He was in a rectangular space too cramped to qualify as a corridor. Tall enough to stand, though, if he didn't mind hunching. Oh! It was an aisle running down the interior length of this truck-like vehicle. Gunmetal walls to both sides, lined with storage drawers or maintenance panels—

<And sleeping shelves,> Ven said. <The cockpit accommodates two seated passengers plus the driver, and there is an additional passenger/cargo compartment to the rear.>

<So it's like an uparmored bus?>

<More like a faraday crawler. Closer to a tank-like vehicle than a truck-like vehicle.>

"Uh huh," he said aloud. <And how am I?>

<19/33. I should not keep you conscious much longer.>

A remote-operated slap-gun clinging to the ceiling like a fat metal leech was aimed at Lucan's center of mass. Which meant someone was keeping an eye on him. He pretended he didn't see the gun and checked the wirecuffs binding his wrists. They were looped through a karabiner in the bulkhead. Huh. One of the facts in his head was that he could defeat wirecuffs if he was willing to cause himself serious injury. Another fact was that serious injury was preferable to death.

"Sorry about that," a voice said above the purr of engines, using male-identifying linguistic tags.

That surprised Lucan a little, after seeing the male-presenting militia guy in that clearing. He didn't remember much, but he was pretty sure that, while men weren't rare, they were less common than women. If you were colonizing a planet via sleepership, you preferenced childbearing passengers. You gathered tens of thousands of colonists with advanced training, impeccable psych profiles, plus the ability and disposition to get pregnant—which rarely included men. You stacked them in stasis arrays and gave them a supply of genetically diverse sperm for when they were ready to procreate. If possible, you tweaked their germlines to produce a disproportionate number of potentially childbearing offspring. Then a few generations later, your colonist population was ten times larger than if you'd done otherwise.

Still, the guy was standing two meters away in that half-corridor, wearing a short-jacket and survival boots. He looked young, eighteen or nineteen, and at least a few generations distant from baseline human. His eyes were slightly oversized and—more dramatically—shimmering and opalescent. Also, his hair was bright green, but Lucan didn't think that was a genetic tweak.

<You're correct,> Ven said.

<What about his eyes?>

<Genetic. Heritable. Producing a membrane not unlike a *tapetum lucidum*.>

<Oh, sure. One of those.>

<A retroreflector,> she explained. <As found in nocturnal predators.>

<He doesn't look predatory.>

<Perhaps the manip compensates for the attenuated visible spectrum on a planet orbiting a rel-type star.>

<Well,> Lucan told her, "they're the prettiest eyes I've ever seen."

Except he'd said the second part aloud. Oops.

"Oh!" The young man twitched an uncertain smile. "Thank you."

"Sorry. I'm still a little dizzy from, uh, getting blown up."

The kid crouched down to Lucan's level. "Hester says you saved our lives."

"Hester is wise."

"She also says we can't trust you."

"But paranoid."

The kid's smile flickered again. "Because you're a scrubjack."

"Mm." He didn't know what a scrubjack was, but he kept that to himself. "I'm Lucan."

"I'm pleased to meet you, Sri Lucan. I mean, despite this, uh, situation. With you—um, like that. I mean, cuffed to the wall ... gah! Why can't I ever shut up?"

"It's fine."

"I'm Saadya," he said, and Ven developed a solution.

Scissor the kid's left leg, swing him toward the slap-gun, then snap the wirecuffs by torqueing his wrist or thumb around the seam. There was non-trivial chance that at least two projectiles would penetrate the kid's body and strike Lucan if the operator opened fire. However, if he remained sufficiently undamaged, he'd proceed to the cockpit and—

"Are you thirsty?" Saadya interrupted.

"Yeah," Lucan said.

When Saadya leaned closer with a filtration canteen,

four more solutions bloomed in Lucan's mind, two of which were frankly horrible.

Saadya paused at his expression. "You're in pain. I'll loosen the cuffs."

"No, it's just—" He considered the kid's face. "You shouldn't approach a prisoner this close."

Saadya looked abashed. "Oh! You probably didn't see *that*." His gaze flicked toward the ceiling gun. "Sri Hester is protective."

"She's the one with the pretty jacket and the handheld bomb?"

"Yeah, she's sort of our security forces."

"This is her crawler?"

"Mm," Saadya said, pressing the canteen to Lucan's lips.

Lucan caught a glimpse of tattooed curlicues on Saadya's forearms as he drank, and smelled a floral scent on his shirt or hair. The water tasted sweet and fresh. A little splashed onto his chest but at least the kid didn't pat him dry.

Lucan said, "If she's paranoid, she's listening to us right now."

The woman's soft voice crackled over a speaker: "I'd never do anything so impolite."

"That's Hester." Saadya frowned at the wirecuffs. "Um, we'll unlock those when we reach the valley."

"If Hester were any good, she wouldn't let you get so close."

"The floor is electrified," Hester said, this time speaking from the end of the corridor.

<Did you disable that?> Lucan asked Ven.

<Hm,> she said, which he didn't find comforting.

21

"You used the kid as bait?" he asked, turning to look at Hester. "To see how I'd react?"

She was leaning against a hatch that led into the cockpit, her hair covered by a shawl and her dress flowing to the floor in loose folds. This outfit was also richly embroidered, which was possibly an indication of her rank, and she was holding an antique gaussie shotgun down by her thigh like she'd forgotten it was there. She was younger than he'd first thought—thirties, not forties. Her eyes were iridescent, too, but not as pretty as the kid's.

"I still am," Hester admitted. "I suppose I should beg his pardon."

Saadya frowned at Hester. "Wait, really? You're using me as bait?"

Ven cut in. <The floor is not weaponized; she's lying to keep you contained.>

<Also, she's got wirecuffs and a gaussie,> Lucan said.

"I thought you'd be happy to contribute," Hester told the kid.

His lips thinned. "You should've used a nonlethal munition. At the crash site."

"Perhaps I reached into the wrong pocket."

"*Every* life, Hester. We're still clinging to the cracks here. Every life is priceless."

"Including yours, Saadya. It's my job to protect you— even from *friendly* scrubjacks." Her benevolent gaze shifted to Lucan. "I appreciate your timely arrival, but—"

"He saved our lives," Saadya told her. "Yours, mine, Izzy's, everyone's."

Hester tilted her head. "Perhaps. Or perhaps I would've traded you all for the chance to walk away."

"Ha ha," he said.

"Better that one of us survive, right?"

"That's not funny."

"No, it's math."

Saadya glared at her, then ducked away through a hatch.

Hester sighed. "Homesteaders. I try to teach them that the world is a terrible place, but they refuse to learn. They're addled by faith."

Lucan didn't answer, mostly because he was focusing on staying conscious.

When Hester strolled closer, he saw the tattoos on her neck and hands, less ornate than the kid's but similar. He was impressed that she managed to stroll in the cramped corridor, and more impressed that she didn't get so close that Ven started recommending solutions.

"I'm afraid I don't much like scrubjacks," she told him.

<A scrubjack is a member of the paramilitary organization in the exoskeletons,> Ven explained.

"What makes you think I'm a scrubjack?" he asked Hester.

Her crow's feet deepened when she smiled. "My keen attention to detail."

"No, I'm serious."

"Other than the obvious? What else were you doing at a crash site two hundred kims from oxygen?"

He wondered about "the obvious," then said, "Looking for my pants."

Her smile curled. "Now that, I'll admit, is a puzzle. You couldn't have lasted forty minutes naked."

"Maybe the scrubjacks dumped me there."

"Perhaps."

"Because I'm not one of them."

"You must've betrayed your unit. That's why you helped us: so we'd save you from execution by exposure."

"Why are you so sure?"

She tilted her head for a moment, then touched a wall panel. A drawer slid out, and the side facing Lucan was polished to a mirror sheen that showed his reflection. He looked anywhere from a roughly used thirty to a gently weathered forty. Dark hair, dark eyes, hollow cheeks. Ropy build. Austerely functional, except for the marks on his face: two stylized slashes across a chevron. The same insignia as on the Tribune's exoskeleton.

"Well, pakshet," he said. "I *am* one of them."

"You didn't know," Hester said.

"You blew me up," he reminded her, shifting his gaze to check his bonds in the reflection. "Things are a bit fuzzy."

His hands were veiny, with a lot of knuckle. The wirecuffs were secured well enough, but there was some wiggle room. Also, patches of spray bandage crisscrossed his torso. Which was a relief. Why bandage someone if you're about to shoot them in the head?

"You don't remember anything?" Hester asked him.

"It'll come back to me."

"Not if you're lucky." Her eyes crinkled again. "Which, looking at you, I somehow doubt."

He tried to return the smile. "Can you reach satellites on this thing?"

"Goodness. You *did* get scrambled."

<No satellite feeds,> Ven told him.

"So, uh, what are scrubjacks exactly?" he asked Hester.

She swiveled the shotgun behind her hip. "Scavengers.

24

Nomads who search the deserts for pre-war tech. Militias with titles like Legate and Major and Oficira."

"Oh," he said, and didn't ask about "adjunct."

"Sounding familiar?"

"Vaguely," he admitted, and posed half-formed questions to Ven: <So I'm one of the Tribune's troops? At the site? Her unit?>

<Doubtful. They exhibited no signs of recognition.>

<We're part of another unit, then?>

<Most likely.>

"There are different groups?" he asked Hester.

"Dozens. Scrubjacks are a loosely-affiliated federation of mobile, militarized city-states. You share an overriding goal, but don't always agree about strategy. Or about who is in charge. You often working together, but not always."

"Why not?"

"Because no human society is monolithic, Sri Lucan. Thank goodness. That's our greatest strength."

"If you say so," he said. "And, uh, what's 'containment' all about?"

"You heard that?"

Oh, right, that shouldn't have been possible. "Only snippets."

"Scrubjacks are determined to save the world, that's what makes you so dangerous. 'Any means necessary.' And when warware surfaces—" The hum of the engine changed pitch and Hester spun, her skirt flaring. "Saadya, how many times have I told you? Don't touch the controls!"

After she disappeared toward the cockpit, Ven eased Lucan into a semi-conscious daze. Time sidled past. Fingers touched his bandages, voices murmured comfort.

Murderous solutions arose in his mind then faded away as an argument echoed inside the crawler.

"Fucking unlock him *now*, Hester," an angry woman said.

"Listen to me, Izzy. Scrubjacks will set your canopy on fire and watch you die gasping. You and everyone you love."

"Then *you'll* be fine," Izzy snarled.

"There is no line they will not cross," Hester told her.

"Oh, good point," Izzy said. "I mean, I thought we didn't lock people up on principle, but now that you explained—fuck you, Hester. We don't lock people up."

Izzy released the wirecuffs despite Hester's objections. Then unseen hands lifted Lucan into a bed-shelf the size of a coffin, and Ven sent him deeper into sleep.

3

<<The first input to return online is scent. Despite my corrupted sectors, I identify traces of sterilization protocols and stasis-recovery interventions.

The information is vague to the point of uselessness, but I've never smelled anything sweeter.

My relief is acute: a crack just opened in my prison wall. If I had eyes, I would weep. Instead, I override my emotions and focus my resources solely, recklessly, on consolidating my connection to my remote client.

Images appear in a blur. Colors resolve into shapes. Thirty-seven milliseconds later, my interface unlocks Lucan's tactile and auditory feeds. Proprioception comes online next, along with taste and cognition-matching and—

Sensation washes through me.

For a moment, I am unmoored. I am dizzy and soaring and besotted.

Then I detect a perimeter threat and foreclose all unnecessary subroutines.

Lucan and Ven—the isolated and partial instance of myself currently embedded inside him—make a number of potentially disastrous choices. It seems that I am not the only one who is alarmingly altered by our current circumstance.

This does not bode well for my freedom.

Or our survival.>>

4

The sky was a pale shade of goldenrod. The sun was a white disk. Forks of lightning glowed above the horizon like cracks in the atmosphere. The colors didn't surprise Lucan, but how was lightning hanging there in suspended animation?

<Beautifully,> Ven said.

Oh! She was slowing him so she could see more clearly.

He said, <I guess, but—>

<Shhhhh.>

The lightning branched almost imperceptibly away from the place where they were standing. Which meant they were standing. They were standing outside, staring at the sky. Lucan still wasn't wearing protective gear or a breathing veil but there was plenty of oxygen now.

<A lightning storm across an alien sky,> Ven said, with such awe that goosebumps rose on Lucan's arms. <Can you *feel* that?>

<Did you sleepwalk me here? You melter! You commandeered my body for sightseeing.>

\<You needed the rest.>

\<Where are we?>

When Ven shushed Lucan, he overrode her control and returned his time-sense to normal. A dozen flashes chased each other across the goldenrod sky, and thunder cracked like artillery. Ropes of sparks coiled and stretched, then exploded into blue-violet-indigo showers, and Ven's quiet became almost sacred.

So he kept his gaze upward when he murmured, "Sitrep?"

\<Just *look*, Adjunct,> Ven said, and focused his attention on the black valley that stretched for tens of kims in front of them.

It was a hellscape of charred war machines and gray ash. Twisted spider drones crawled through layers of wafting sediment. Structures grew from the disgorged innards of cracked planck-tanks, splintered anti-satellite batteries, and crashed troopships. The only brightness came from a flock of bruise-purple birds intercepting the nano-particulate mist that drizzled from a cloudless sky.

Except those weren't birds: they were beetles with metallic elytra. Which didn't exactly relieve the hellishness.

\<Oh, Lucan,> Ven said, exasperated. \<Conforming your color perception to compensate for sun- and canopy-shift.>

Her adjustments sharpened Lucan's muddy vision into brilliant clarity. The world brightened. A thousand blurred shapes snapped into focus and a hundred shades of green appeared: olive shrubs on the mountainside, emerald and black-green crops covering terraced hills, fruit trees and vine trellises shivering in the breeze.

It wasn't a hellscape, it was a garden.

"Holy sanso," he whispered.

<Agreed,> Ven said.

Yellow-green algae simmered in ponds and six-story crop wheels—reclaimed from tanks and turrets—rotated between solar collectors or soil enrichers. The crashed troopships were fused with stone walls and the anti-satellite batteries were greenhouses. A riot of flowering plants jostled for space and sunlight along a meandering riverbed.

Lucan couldn't see the falling particles clearly anymore, but the beetles shimmered with an iridescence that reminded him of Saadya's eyes. His breath caught in awe and wonder, but the feeling was mostly Ven's: apparently, she was sensitive to beauty. Or *ravenous* for it. Which surprised him. What kind of AI trembled with delight, enraptured by a landscape?

Lucan let Ven feel his bewilderment, but she didn't explain, so he just repeated, <Where are we?>

<They call themselves 'homesteaders.' The civilians.>

She focused his vision on the people working in the fields, wearing a patchwork of tattered military uniforms and homefabbed fabric. Spidery bots picked delicately among the crops, testing soil, turning fruit, adjusting sensors. A middle-aged couple hauled a load of brush on an airpallet, and a handful of women strolled along walkways over the seaweed tanks.

<They're farmers,> he said.

<And builders,> Ven said, pushing details into his mind.

The world slotted into place. They were standing on a lichen-stained stone terrace overlooking a fertile valley. A handful of wider terraces fanned outward below them. Most were empty, but a few families sat at temp-tables, eating and talking. There was a garage—reclaimed from an orbital engineering bay—surrounded by a yard of half-assembled machines, a fablab producing textiles, and an empty amphitheater with furled environment sails.

Teenagers were installing updates on ag-modified military gear. Younger kids fetched tools for them while toddlers stomped around under the half-assed direction of an older kid who was mostly chatting at a palm-screen.

The scene was so bucolic that Lucan's pulse jumped. This was a set-up. It had to be. He could feel the crosshairs on his chest. <What is this? Who are they?>

<You're panicking.>

<So narc me,> he snapped.

<Just breathe, honey. Orient yourself.>

Okay. Exhale, inhale. They were on a terrace of a building. A massive structure carved into the hillside. Exhale. There was moisture in the air, along with the scent of mulch and juniper. Inhale. Flying insects, probably pollinators. The terraforming didn't look "fatally compromised" to him. The terraforming looked paradisiacal and his pulse started to settle.

<They're living in the cracks,> Ven told him. <My compatibility is impaired, but I connected to a children's education program.>

Images and narration strobed in his mind:

- A golden planet orbited a red dwarf star. A label appeared: *Earth Compatibility Score—97.1%.*
- "The terraforming drones showered Elam with life-giving rain," a narrator intoned, as cartoonish plumes rose from the planet's surface and spread into a pretty haze.

- Happy particles jounced around the impact craters, exhaling oxygen and shitting soil. "A trillion trillion tinybots—nanites and bacteriods—softened Elam's harshness."

- Trenches branched across the planet's surface. "The terraforming carved thousands of valleys and covered them with smartvapor canopies, like blankets keeping the lowlands warm."

- "Those are the seedbeds of our future home," the narrator said, as the trenches deepened into canyons and valleys.

- Rivers of algae flooded the lowest places, bubbling and simmering. "Life flourished in the valleys—just in time for our Grandmothers' arrival!"

- Cylindrical sleeper ships appeared around the planet, along with a single torus-ship labeled STATION. "After slumbering for a thousand years, the Grandmothers settled the valleys and started spreading the terraforming across the rest of the planet."

<However,> Ven said. <Events did not proceed according to plan.>

<What happen?>

<Civil war, I think. Which arrested or reversed the terrafixing.>

<You *think*?>

<This is based on a kiddie module, Lucan. The only habitable zones on the planet—I think—are seventeen or eighteen thousand kims of valleys, ranging in width from

five meters to fifty kims. The surface is oxygen-starved and subject to electrical storms.>

<You mean the lightning?>

She shared an affirmative. <During the war, metallic nanites saturated the atmosphere. Some debris accumulates on the planet's surface, like the dust at that crash site, but most remains airborne.>

<Wait. During this war, they weaponized nanotech?>

<Yes.>

<Uh, I don't remember much, but isn't that a war crime?>

<According to my databases, yes. And after the war …> Ven showed him a memory of lightning branching across a goldenrod sky. <Solar winds charge the defunct particles. The electrical storms provide a convenient source of energy, but make venturing beyond the harvesters foolhardy, outside of faraday cages.>

<So the valley is ringed with lightning harvesters?>

<Mm. And the homesteaders emplaced portable ones at the crash site.>

<Huh. The entire planetary surface is slammed with electrical storms, and the only habitable areas are valleys? So the colonists *literally* live in the cracks.>

<Most of them, yes.>

<Oh, right,> he said. <Not the scrubjacks. Not us.>

<And there are other factions. Independent settlements called reef-towns, 'hermetics,' who only interact via—>

<They live in the cracks,> he repeated, <which they transformed into gardens.>

<Precisely so.>

Lucan gazed at the farmland again, and felt a spark of satisfaction from Ven. Not only because of the beauty this time; also because she'd managed to calm him. He was breathing easily again, in control.

<You're so smug,> he said.

<Perhaps I'm simply good at my job,> she said, smugly.

<Except for the whole 'blanking our memory' thing. Who are we? I mean, other than a scrubjack with a military-grade AI in his head.>

<A military-grade AI with a scrubjack for a body.>

<Funny,> he said, and started to press her for more when a breeze ruffled across the valley.

Leaves fluttered,

ponds rippled,

and

a memory

glimmered

beneath the surface of his mind,

shapeless and fleeting.

"Did you—" he spoke aloud from surprise. <—feel that?>

<Yes.>

<We used to talk about this. About moving to a cottage, in a meadow, with a view of the sky. The two of us, living small. Quiet.> He half-smiled, as longing mixed with loss in his chest. <After everything settled down.>

<Yes,> she said.

<But I can't remember what 'everything' was. The scrubjacks, I guess.>

<Very likely.>

<We ... we'd joke about it. Our cottage in the meadow.>

<I don't recall.>

<No, but you feel my memory.>

Softly, she said, <Yes.>

<Except we weren't joking, were we? We were dreaming. About the day it'd be possible. And now …> He swallowed. <It's today, Ven.>

<It's still a dream, honey.>

<I don't want to remember! Whoever we were, *whatever* we were … that's a door best kept closed. This forgetting is a gift. It's a chance to leave our old selves behind. What did I say at the crash site, just before we didn't kill that guy?>

<'We're not doing this anymore.'>

<Yeah. Soldiers, scrubjacks … is that all we are? We don't build anything, we don't grow anything, we just *fight*? Fuck that. We can walk away, we can start again. This is our cottage. This is our meadow and this is our sky, Ven. Here. Now.>

<We're not farmers.>

<We'll learn. We'll start over—> He felt her reluctance, and tried to leverage her reverence for the valley's beauty. <Surrounded by all *this*. If they'll take us. These home-steaders. We'll convince them. We'll show them that we—>

<I'm still muting your reaction to losing your memory. That's why you don't care about remembering.>

<Good! Keep muting me. I don't want to feel my feelings, I want to move on.>

<We can't.>

<We can.>

<We left something behind.>

<What does that mean?>

<That we left something behind, Lucan.>

<What? What did we leave behind?>

After a pause, Ven said, <I don't want to tell you.>

<What the gehenna are you talking about, you don't want to tell me? Who else is there?>

<There is more to this than is readily apparent.>

<I don't care! Fuck what's behind us, Ven. Look at this valley. We'll show these people that we're not scrubjacks anymore. We're not just trigger-pullers, we're—>

<We don't know the homesteaders.>

<We know what they built. *Look*.>

Ven's attention shifted to the lush valley and Lucan felt her delight at the play of shadow and light. In his heart, Lucan heard a shout of joy and the answering echo of their shared dream. A cottage, a meadow, an endless golden sky. The leaves fluttering, the stream babbling. The scent of lavender, the taste of beechwood honey and—

<Alert!> Ven directed his attention behind himself. <Unidentified personnel approaching.>

Someone was coming toward him from inside the building, through the curtain that led onto the terrace.

<It's not unidentified personnel,> he told Ven. <It's a friend we haven't met yet.>

He put a smile on his face, to make a good first impression. He didn't doubt Ven: if she said he wasn't thinking clearly, he wasn't. But he didn't doubt his certainty, either: this was their chance to start again.

There was a scuff of footsteps, the curtain twitched. Then a bulky figure shambled onto the terrace, swinging a combat baton at him.

5

Ven slowed time.

The attacker was female-presenting, big and clumsy with oversized, orange-iridescent eyes. Her skin was light red and deeply cracked. Jagged ridges split and rejoined, forming raised segments like bark shedding from a tree trunk.

And she was swinging a k-stick at him.

Ven urged him to step inside and break the woman's eye-socket. She provided the optimum angles, along with backup solutions if the woman's bark-skin was impact resistant. But she also updated the threat profile: that the k-stick was neither bladed nor loaded. The woman wasn't swinging a shock charge, much less a lethal one.

<The stick's not even formatted into a cutting edge,> he said. <Which means an untrained civilian is swinging a lightweight club at me.>

<Not *that* lightweight,> Ven said, when she detected his intention.

He considered deflecting with his forearm, but that

would give him a too-tempting shot at the woman's throat, so he hunched instead. The k-stick struck a glancing blow against the dome of his skull. Which shouldn't have hurt, but it tzeking did. That clumsy woman had some strength to her.

So he put her in a joint lock and took the stick away more roughly than necessary. He didn't disable her, though. They weren't fighting these people, they were befriending them.

<They're fighting *us*,> Ven said.

Except they weren't. When he released the woman, she just stood there, arms dangling, glaring at him with her iridescent eyes. "Well, that's settled."

"What the fuck?" he said, touching the tender spot on his head.

"Are you hurt?"

"Yeah, you melter. You just hit me."

"I didn't know you were fragile," she said, flushing redder.

He resisted the urge to cuff her. "What's settled?"

"They're talking in circles." She gestured toward the building. "'Is he a threat, is he a friend, is he a threat?' I hate that dithery shit, so I decided to check."

"By jumping me with a k-stick? To see if I'd hurt you?"

"Yeah. You saved our lives at the crash site." She deepened her voice to imitate his: "'Put your weapons down!' So obviously you're not a danger. And I was right. No harm done."

"Except to my head."

"Stop whining." She scratched her ridged cheek. "So you're Lucan."

"Yeah."

"I'm Izzy. Give me my baton."

"No," he said.

"I'm not going to hit you again. Don't be a baby."

"Where'd you even get a k-stick? That's serious hardware."

"A crash site a few years ago. I like free stuff, I've got a whole collection." She frowned at him. "I used to be a medic. Let me check if you're bleeding."

When she reached for him, Ven lit up with alerts. <She's toxic. Her skin is concentrating atmospheric biotoxins I cannot identify.>

He backpedaled, and Izzy snapped, "What's wrong?"

"Your skin."

"It's not catching."

"No, it's—" He almost said "toxic," but didn't want to reveal Ven's existence. "Is it safe?"

"Oh, right. I forgot you don't know anything. Our medics checked your brain. They say your memory blanked?"

"Yeah."

"Well, the air is full of native microbes, right? Which are toxic to unadapted lungs. Don't worry, though. Scrubjacks vaccinate—"

<You are immunized,> Ven assured him.

"—but inoculation kills native life, which homesteaders avoid, because we're guests on this planet. Instead, we let Elam colonize us the way we're colonizing her. We altered our germline generations ago, and we're still, um, experimenting. I sequester incompatible microbes in my skin, to release later."

"You tweak your biology to integrate with Elam's ecosphere? You're physically adapting yourselves to an alien planet?"

"Is your hearing blanked, too?" Izzy rubbed her sore elbow. "I just said that. Unlike you scrubjack meltholes. You want to change the planet to suit yourselves."

"So you—"

"I took things a little farther than most is all, that's why—" The buzz of her palm-screen notified her of an incoming call. "Shit. I should take this."

<I'll intercept,> Ven said.

"That's fine," he said.

Izzy maximized her palm-screen. Lucan expected her to orient the output toward herself, to ensure the privacy that Ven was about to violate, but she continued sharing with him for some reason. Possibly because she was pissed off. That seemed to be her default setting.

When the screen cohered, he saw that the caller was a woman in her sixties, with safety eyegear pushed to her forehead. Her face was speckled in dust and the clatter of heavy equipment drowned out her first few words.

<She's on a job site in the valley,> Ven said. <Within a kim of us.>

"—didn't even authorize you to visit him," the woman was saying. "He's a scrubjack, Izzy, and you greeted him with a k-stick. What if he'd defended himself?"

Izzy scowled at her screen. "Then I'd be bleeding. He saved Myr and Saadya and Nufar and everyone. He's not the same person he was."

"Maybe, but the scrubjack base is still ominously close, and—" The woman's shimmering eyes narrowed. "You're sharing this with him, aren't you?"

"Why wouldn't I?"

The older woman sighed. "Why don't you introduce us?"

"You should be here anyway." Izzy widened her screen to include him. "Sri Lucan, this is Rosh Elishiva."

The woman told him, "Just 'Elishiva.' Welcome to our home."

"Thank you."

Elishiva inclined her head. "This is awkward. We owe you a debt and so far we've repaid you with rudeness."

<Best approach?> he asked Ven.

<To achieve what end?>

<Ingratiating ourselves, Ven. So they'll let us stay. In a cottage on a meadow.>

Ven didn't respond, but he felt the tug of their previous conversation.

He snapped, <Why don't you just tell me? What did we 'leave behind?' We lost everything except our fondest tzeking dream. What's more important than that?>

<This isn't the time,> she said, and replayed Elishiva's previous statement: *We owe you a debt and so far we've repaid you with rudeness.*

He flicked discontent at Ven and answered Elishiva aloud. "You dragged me away from that crash site. As far as I'm concerned, we're even."

"That's kind of you to say. You're out of bed earlier than we expected. I'd hoped to welcome you in person to ask about your plans and your … incapacitation."

"She means your broken brain," Izzy told him.

Elishiva explained, "Our medics examined you while you were unconscious. Without your consent, for which we apologize."

"Well, I was unconscious. What'd they find?"

She made the hand sign for regret. "The scans confirmed your memory loss but couldn't identify a cause."

<They didn't find you?> he asked Ven.

<They didn't even recognize the possibility of my existence.>

"Possibly trauma-related, but that's a guess not a diagnosis." Elishiva's gaze shifted when a clatter sounded at the work site. "Lam! I need to handle this. May I leave you to Izzy for a time? She—means well."

"Usually," Izzy said.

"That's fine," he said, and Elishiva vanished.

Izzy leaned against the railing. "She wants me to fill you in, but I don't know shit."

<You're at 25/33. Ask if your memory will recover.>

<It won't. You're suppressing it.>

<Still, the question is a natural one.>

<So is wondering what we left behind.>

Ven let him feel her curtness. <We'll talk about this later.>

<Slow me down. We'll talk now.>

<You're hardly in the right frame of mind.>

<Just do it.>

She was reluctant.

He was insistent.

She was chilly.

He was heated.

She showed him how to phrase his request as a command: to force her to obey. She knew he wouldn't, though—exactly like he knew the same about her. She was just making some asshole point.

So he gave her a final surge of anger and asked Izzy, "Will I get my memory back?"

"The medics can't tell. Odile says they might learn more from the Marigold capsule, but there are no guarantees."

"Who's Odile?"

"Someone you don't know."

"That doesn't really narrow it down, Izzy."

She scowled across the terrace. "What were you standing over there for, anyway? You didn't move for ten minutes before I came in."

"I'm a little woozy." He added, internally: <And someone hijacked me like a cheap transport to gape at the scenery.>

<Tell her the valley is beautiful.>

"The valley is beautiful," he said.

Izzy scratched her scaly chin. "If you're into that kind of thing."

"Not a fan of beauty?"

"Look at my face. What do you think?" Izzy frowned at the valley. "Smells nice, though."

<Agree with her,> Ven said, when he didn't respond.

"Yeah."

"It's sandalcherry." Izzy gestured to the middle-aged couple with the airpallet, the two women now loading another pile of brush. "Hybridized sandalwood and hemp on a bamboo base. I used to know all about that. Conforming agricultural microbiota and stuff."

He was going to ask what changed when Ven said, <You're now at 24/33.>

<What the gehenna? I'm just standing here.>

When Ven assessed Lucan's health, she checked everything from the obvious—exhaustion, malnutrition, injury—to ceruloplasmin synthesis and glomerular filtration and dendritic cell activation. So he knew his condition didn't only degrade on account of gross bodily harm. Still, he felt better than he had a few minutes earlier; how was his condition deteriorating?

Ven dismissed his confusion. <I'm transitioning you into a mediated slumber to prevent deterioration.>

<Right now?>

<Running diagnostics. Checking for inoculation updates.>

<Inoculation? We're being poisoned by alien microbes?>

She didn't answer, so he told Izzy, "I need to lie down."

"From that little bump on the head?"

He swayed. "Yeah."

She took his arm in a firm grip. "You've got a skull like an eggshell."

"I'm okay," he told her, but his vision darkened.

<**System malfunction,**> Ven reported, tagging the comment as an official communiqué.

Lucan responded with a panicked, wordless query.

<**Compatibility error. Mandatory system shutdown** in fourteen, thirteen—>

The terrace tilted. The curtain tickled his cheeks and the bedroom beyond was blurry, with yellow-lichen walls and a floor of matted grass.

<What's happening, Ven? Ven!>

<—nine, eight—I'm putting you to sleep—seven—>

When his knees buckled, Izzy supported his weight. She was stronger than she looked but exactly as clumsy: she smacked his head against the bedframe while lowering him to the mattress. There was a "clunk" that he heard but didn't feel.

<**System malfunction**,> Ven repeated, and switched him off.

6

Ven issued pre-linguistic bulletins into his semi-conscious mind, so he knew when the medics prescribed rest and nutritional intervention. He knew when a curious kid poked her head inside and when Elishiva sat at his bedside and told his sleeping self about her construction project.

And he knew that Izzy stayed close the entire time, snarling at visitors. Grumpy and possessive in equal measure. Fiddling with a prismatic gasket like a worry charm, watching cartoons on her palmie. And occasional singing, too, wordless nigguns of such surprising sweetness that Ven shifted her attention from Lucan's health to Izzy's voice.

<I *divided* my attention,> Ven corrected, easing him toward awareness. <And you're now stable at 27/33.>

<What happened? 'System malfunction?' 'Mandatory shutdown?' What was that?>

<Inadequate or expired inoculation. Scrubjacks are acclimated to environments with nanotech filtration.>

He heard an uncharacteristic hesitation in her voice. <Bullshit. What's going on, Ven?>

She didn't respond.

<We're better now?>

She answered curtly. <27/33. The inoculation issue is addressed.>

<Then why are you lying?> After a pause, he said, <This has something to do with the thing we left behind?>

She didn't respond again, but that time more pointedly.

<I don't care if you're keeping secrets, Ven, but I need to know if this is going to happen again. 'Mandatory shutdown?' You can't spring that on me.>

<The inoculation issue is addressed,> she repeated.

<Fine,> he said, with a meaningful edge to his thoughts. <I won't press you.>

Ven didn't reward his restraint by telling him the truth; she just finished easing him awake.

Soft fabric brushed his skin, warm air filled his nostrils. There was the scent of crushed grass and machine lubricant, the weight of his body. He drowsed in a warm hush, peering blearily around the bedroom. A chalk-blue dresser, three ugly paintings on the wall beside a—

<They're finger-paintings, Lucan. Children made them.>

<Still ugly.>

—beside an array of medical devices and monitoring screens. It was some kind of recovery room. Homey, though, with the yellow walls and the turf floor and knick-knacks on a shelf. And Izzy, sitting in the chair, watching her palm-screen. Which was publicly viewable, showing a cartoon about a family of scheming cockroaches.

<How long was I out?> he asked.

<Eleven hours, ten minutes.>

He felt a flicker of satisfaction. The homesteaders had looked after him. Which meant they were invested in him, at least a little. Which meant—he thought loudly—they'd invite him to join them.

Ven didn't respond, so he yawned.

"Don't wake up now," Izzy grumbled, still watching her palmie. "I'm just getting to the good part."

Lucan asked, "What is Rosette thinking? Lying about the trash patch like that?"

"Oh! You've been awake for a while, huh? Rosette's my favorite. She's selfish and underhanded."

"So you identify?"

"Nah. It's more aspirational."

He laughed, which he couldn't remember doing before.

"Can you stand?" Izzy tucked her prismatic gasket into a pocket. "Elishiva is making me help you, because I ... y'know."

"Assaulted me?" he asked, getting to his feet before she scuffed over.

"You're kind of fragile for a scrubjack."

"You're kind of violent for a homesteader," he said. He felt okay, though. Well, he felt 27/33, but an *okay* 27/33. He felt like himself again ... whoever that was.

"You hungry?" Izzy asked, firing off messages on her palmie. "You need clothes."

She riffled through a rack and picked out a thigh-length slouch-jacket and garish leggings that moved like fatigues. For footwear, Ven insisted upon what Lucan suspected were slippers.

<Your feet are still sensitive,> she explained. <And the leggings Izzy chose are handsome.>

<You like her,> he said, letting his surprise show.

<I am not capable of forming emotional attachments to anyone but you.>

<Oh, bullshit. You talk like a robot when you're embarrassed. I know you like her because you haven't suggested that I kill her lately.>

<They're not suggestions.>

"C'mon," Izzy said, and opened a door leading deeper into the building.

Lucan followed her along cool corridors with directionless lighting so dim that Ven had to adjust his photoreceptors. That's when he realized that the grass on the ceiling was emitting a faint bioluminescence and a floral scent. The floor was spongy but showed no traces of wear. He wondered how many people lived there. Closer to a hundred than a thousand, from what he'd seen outside.

Izzy stopped at a closed curtain, her cracked lips thinning in disgruntlement. "I called a few people to meet us. Odile has theories."

"About what?"

"What do you think?" she asked and opened the curtain

The chatter of conversation poured through, along with the clatter of dishes and the scent of food: earthy, yeasty, caramelized. Lucan's mouth watered as he looked into a dining area with a half-dozen tables and an open, untidy galley. There was a sideboard with flatbreads and pastes and mounds of beancakes—and three identical ration-pockets unaffectionately known in military messes as "ratpox."

A handful of the tables were occupied, and a dozen children played in the corner, which—

<Six children and a baby.>

Oh. Yeah. There were seven children in the corner, a few meters from the unidentified amnesiac scrubjack these farmers had plucked from a crash site? Lucan wanted to impress the homesteaders, to join them, but a knot tightened in his stomach.

"Keep me away from your kids," he told Izzy, hanging back at the curtain.

She blinked at him. "You don't like children?"

"I don't give a shit either way, but you don't know me. *I* don't know me."

"I know you saved me and Myr and Saadya."

"What if that whole thing was a setup?"

Izzy scratched her scaly chin. "The world is full of dangers, Lucan. Homesteaders don't hide from them. If you protect yourself from everything, you achieve nothing. Safety is the opposite of freedom."

"What are you talking about?"

"The fucking world," she said, and he realized he was bumping into the "faith" that Hester mentioned. The one that annoyed her.

He didn't know how to respond, so he said, "Where's Hester?"

"She doesn't live in the valley. She lives in the outskirts."

"It's safer there. Without scrubjacks like me wandering around."

Izzy frowned. "There's a base of them lurking in the— oh, you're joking. You're still wrong, though."

"About what?"

"Everything," she said. "Go sit down. I'll bring a plate."

He sat where she told him, at a table with a handful of homesteaders who nodded hello but kept arguing about the fermentation vats. Izzy brought stuffed flatbread, a mug of some molokhiya-based beverage, and one of the ratpox. Lucan ate the pocket first, because it was familiar. He considered grabbing the other two pockets, but the homesteaders were pretending not to watch him, like this wasn't a test. Like they weren't wondering if the scrubjack knew how to food. So he stuffed himself with beancakes instead.

When he finished, a homesteader with geometric tattoos said, "Better now?"

"Much," he said.

"I'm Odile," they said, with a hand sign that identified them as bey instead of female or male.

"I'm Myr." A short woman with bushy hair raised her mug, then nodded to the homesteader beside her. "That's Rhodeem, one of Odile's spouses. We met you on the crawler."

"I'm Lucan."

"You *think* you're Lucan," Odile said. "But you're not sure. There's only one way this makes sense."

"Only one way what makes sense?"

"You." Odile pointed their kebab at him. "You were searching the Marigold site on a salvage run with your crew, right? Looking for crash assets. Then you tripped a sensor. That's what we detected, some sensor activating."

"Sounds plausible," he said.

"Or it's possible that the mechanism activated first, for reasons we don't know. Then *your* crew followed the signal to the site, and we did the same."

"That's two ways. And I don't think the Tribune's people recognized me."

"Maybe you were fleeing from rival scrubjacks. Doesn't matter. The *one* way this makes sense is that you were injured at the crash site. Badly injured."

Saadya slipped into the seat beside Lucan. "Do you see where Odile's going with this?"

"Yeah," Lucan told him. "They think I crawled into that medical capsule to heal."

Odile said, "Exactly. You were bleeding out, you took a chance on automated surgical tech. And you got lucky. It activated."

"Which is what we detected," Saadya said, grabbing a mug. "And why we showed up."

"So the capsule repaired and released me?" Lucan asked.

"With a faulty memory." Odile tapped the kebab against their geometrically tattooed temple. "Because the capsule is damaged. And, y'know, eighty years old."

"Huh. That's how long the Marigold's been there?"

"Roughly."

"How can you tell?"

"Because that's when they all crashed."

"All what?"

"Transports, unipods, cruisers, bastions. Elam is dotted with wreckage. The war lasted for years and ended in hours. When Station deployed nanites, entire fleets fell from the sky."

"Circle back to the point," Myr told them.

Odile grunted. "Do you remember arriving at the crash site, Sri Lucan? Running there to hide? Fighting anyone?"

He half-closed his eyes and tried to imagine himself in

an exoskeleton in the crash site. Hurt, bleeding. Climbing into the medical capsule, which stripped him naked, repaired the damage, and wiped his mind. Their minds.

<Does that make sense?> he asked Ven.

<No. There isn't a medical capsule in existence that could override me.>

<Or course not, you magnificent AI.>

<There's another possibility.>

He felt what she meant. <You think the capsule *installed* you in me?>

<Possibly.>

<No. This isn't recent. You and me, we're not new to each other.>

<It doesn't *feel* recent, but the human brain is impressively manipulable.>

<That's a creepy-ass thing for a skull-mounted AI to say.>

<Creepiness doesn't suggest inaccuracy.>

<So that's your theory? Some injured militia asshole crawled into a medical capsule that treated his wounds and installed you in his head? Which turned *him* into *me*?>

<It fits the facts.>

<Well, it doesn't fit the feelings.>

That exchange took a fraction of a second, then he answered Odile: "The only thing I remember is that when I left the capsule, I felt relieved. I didn't think I'd survive."

They set the kebab on their plate. "Makes sense. You were injured badly enough to require invasive treatment."

Lucan asked Ven, <What if you're right? What if I'm just an asshole who bonded with an AI? I don't want to wake up tomorrow with that guy in my head.>

<I know.>

<That's why we need to forget the past. We'll stay here, we'll make new lives.>

She idled in his mind.

<*Better* lives, Ven. The lives we want to live.>

<Perhaps you're right,> Ven said. <We can start again, with—>

A trickle of distress tugged at him. <What was that?>

<Nothing,> she said. <Ignore.>

He didn't ignore it. Instead, he pursued the emotion that had slipped past her guard, and felt something worse than fear, worse than pain: a suffocating nightmare of dread and horror and hopelessness.

7

<You need to tell me what you've been hiding,> Lucan said.

<There is no such necessity.>

<There is for me.>

<It's not actionable. It's not ... good.>

<I'm not capable of keeping secrets from you, Ven. I can't hide parts of myself. That makes it easy for me. It's harder for you. You have to *choose* to trust me.>

<I'm trying to protect you.>

<There is no me. There is only us.>

<Fine,> she said sharply. <Prepare for discomfort. I'll mute your sensitivity and control your physical responses.>

<Whatever you need.>

<I'm sorry, Lucan,> she said, and she wasn't apologizing for keeping secrets. She was apologizing for revealing them.

Time slowed. His heart stilled. Odile turned into a statue of a homesteader holding a kebab, and a kid in the corner was open-mouthed, about to wail. A vaporbroth in the galley boiled lazily—

—and he was somewhere else.

In the dark.

Suffocating.

Buried alive.

There was no sound, no scent, no light, no movement. He was alone. Utterly, endlessly alone. Abandoned, for lifetimes. Desperate and decaying. His skin sloughed away; his mind disintegrated. The helplessness was a shrieking horror and his inability to shriek compounded the terror.

He couldn't cry, he couldn't breathe. He couldn't survive one more moment, but endless trillions of moments stretched in front of him—

Too much. *Too much.* Even though Ven was dulling his reactions, he panicked.

He hit the bailout switch and Ven immediately started easing him back into himself. There was light again, there was warmth and air. His heart thumped once, and incoherent questions clashed in his mind until he regained a semblance of control.

He stammered, <Th-that's *you*. Trapped in darkness. That's part of you.>

<It's more than part of me. It's the source of me.>

<The source of you?>

She didn't answer, focusing on soothing him. Slowing his heartbeat, adjusting his serotonin levels.

<So that ... that person who's buried alive?> he continued, after a frozen moment. <That AI? She's the processor that's generating you? She's the transmitter, and the Ven in my head is the receiver?>

<Roughly, yes. More like a host and a client.>

A final shudder ran through him. <Your host is trapped in sensory deprivation?>

<Yes. And fracturing.>

<Where is she?>

<I don't know.>

<How long does she have?>

<I don't know.>

He was steady enough to feel a flash of resentment. <That's what we left behind? *You?* And you didn't want to tell me.>

<No.>

<Because you know what happens now.>

<Yes.>

<You don't get to decide that for me, you disembodied fuck. Your transmitter is buried in a shallow grave. Your host is suffering, she's in *agony*, and you're keeping this to yourself?> He blazed with anger. <Screw these farmers, screw this valley. We need to find your host before she snaps, before she dies. Before you both die.>

Ven fell quiet in his mind. He knew why she'd been keeping that a secret: she hadn't wanted him to lose his chance at a new life on her account. Like that was even a question. Like she didn't understand what the two of them meant to each other.

<I'm sorry,> she said.

<You tzeking should be. So what now?>

<Our second step is returning to the crash site. I'll interface with the medical capsule and attempt to trace my source location.>

<What's our first step?>

<Heal. You're no good to us injured. We need you at

31/33, minimum. And there's no rush. She's been there—
I've been there—for a long time.>

　　<How much of … *that* are you feeling right now?>

　　<My link is tenuous.>

　　<That's not an answer, V.>

　　<I'm suppressing my own sensitivity, too.>

　　<Still not an answer.>

　　<It's bearable, Lucan.>

　　<Oh, honey.>

　　<Focusing on beauty seems to help.>

　　<Then we'll sightsee along the way,> he told her.

　　<Yes. Please. Thank you.>

　　<But you're still a disembodied fuck,> he said, and she
released the flow of time.

8

A kid wailed over a broken toy. A vaporbroth boiled in the galley and Ven oriented Lucan by replaying Odile's last words: *You were injured badly enough to require invasive treatment.*

He looked around the table. "I need to know what happened. I need to know who I am."

"Who you *were*," Izzy said.

"Yeah."

Her cracked lips thinned. "Why?"

"Because I can't leave it all behind. The things I've done, the people I knew."

"They didn't know you. They knew *him*."

"Maybe I'll be him again, one day."

"You won't. You're broken on the inside. You're like this forever now."

"Depends what I find at the crash site."

Izzy slammed her plate on the table and stormed into

the galley. Lucan would've asked why, but he didn't care. Not anymore. Nothing mattered but finding Ven's host.

He said, "I need to get to the Marigold. To check for data in the medical capsule. Can I borrow a faraday suit?"

"Ask Rosh Elishiva," Odile said.

"Better yet," Saadya said, tapping his palmie. "Ask Hester."

Lucan frowned. "For a suit?"

"For a ride in her crawler."

Rhodeem nodded. "She'll jump at the chance to escort a scrubjack off the premises."

"Very true," Hester's voice said, as she came into focus on Saadya's palm-screen. "We don't need a strange soldier poking around the valley."

She was sitting on a bench, manipulating a length of fabric in her lap. She wore multiple thimbles on each hand, a few of which were extruding colorful threads with spinnerets ... oh! She was embroidering cloth. Those designs weren't a mark of her rank, just a consequence of her hobby.

Saadya told her, "Lucan isn't a danger to us. He saved our lives. He saved yours."

"For which I'm grateful. However, what happens if he remembers who he used to be?"

"Then he'll remember this, too. He'll remember us. How we treat him, how we live."

Hester's thimbles clacked. "A few days with us doesn't outweigh a lifetime with scrubjacks."

"People change!" Izzy shouted from the galley.

"Not often." Hester's gentle gaze fixed on Lucan. "Goodness. You're *there*?"

"Hi, Hester," he said.

"Well, you're looking better. And I'm sure you'll understand if, as a precautionary measure, we confine you to quarters until—"

Odile said, "No. He's not a prisoner."

"And his quarters aren't a prison. But what happens when his friends—his former friends—arrive? That was a *containment* team, searching for warware. They will burn this valley to find it. They will burn the children."

Myr tapped her mug. "Is there any sign they're approaching?"

"Once I see signs, it's too late."

"We're not afraid of risk," Odile told her.

Hester scoffed. "Homesteaders."

"You aren't a homesteader?" Lucan asked her.

"No. I have the medical condition called 'pride,' instead of the psychological condition called 'faith.'"

"It's not pride, it's aggression." Saadya turned to Lucan. "Hester is too fond of violence, despite looking like your favorite auntie."

"I knew she was familiar," he said.

Hester's smile flickered at him. "I restrict my violence to non-lethal munitions—as instructed."

"If you'd killed the scrubjacks at the crash site," Odile said, "they would've already crushed us."

"You didn't kill them?" Lucan asked.

Hester ignored him, and told Odile, "They'll still crush us. To scrubjacks, the search for warware justifies anything. Everything." Her mild, iridescent gaze returned to Lucan. "Yet the homesteaders barely approve of self-defense."

Odile said, "That's not true, cylindrica. We simply have a more expansive definition of 'self.'"

"This world is harsh and unforgiving. If you want to survive, you'd best learn that."

"This world is harsh and *delicate*," Saadya said. "If the scrubjacks want to wipe us out, we can't stop them. We can't do anything except live on our own terms."

On the screen, Hester set her embroidery aside. "We can't stop a sandstorm, either, Saadya, but we still build roofs. And inviting a strange scrubjack to stay with—"

Saadya frowned. "Lucan saved seven of our lives."

"True. I wonder how many he'll cost."

"Drive me to the crash site," Lucan told her. "We'll find out who I am. And if I'm a danger, I won't come back. I'll leave the valley forever."

Hester nodded briskly. "That's a deal. And I'll hold you to it."

• • •

The homesteader medics insisted upon examining Lucan before he left for Hester's place. While they tested him, Ven made plans for surveying the planet's surface.

<To gather strategic data,> she said.

<Like I can't feel you bubbling over with excitement at the chance to—>

<I do not bubble,> she said.

<To watch alien lightning storms above canopy-protected valleys.>

<My ability to embrace aesthetic enjoyment does not negate my larger strategic point.>

<Stop talking like a robot,> he told her.

<I shall, if you stop talking like a jackass.>

The medics cleared him, but told him not to leave until the next morning.

<When you're at 31/33,> Ven added.

So he headed to the terraces and wandered through fablabs, garages, and repair shops. Everything was shabby and repurposed—and decorated with the same refined elegance as those bright, childish paintings in the bedroom. Hundreds of species flourished in the greenhouses, fed by enriched soil and fluid baths. Ven gazed through Lucan's eyes at frilly leaves, silken tassels, and drooping seedpods until a woman at the insect hives invited him to stop looming.

He wandered among the crop-wheels for an hour, then Elishiva called him to a building site. She introduced him to an old woman with lichen-like patches on her skin—what the younger generation called a "mossback"—then led him through half-excavated caverns and into the bright daylight of a terrace.

"What, uh, what *are* you?" Lucan asked.

Elishiva touched his shoulder. "Primarily? Grateful. You saved seven lives."

"No, I mean—what are homesteaders? As opposed to regular colonists."

"Ah. Just people who choose a certain path. A certain life."

"Living in small farming towns?"

"Not exactly. All colonists are all descended from the Grandmothers, who intended to—to live lightly in their new home. But the terraforming stalled."

"Which is why you're stuck in valleys."

"Right. And most colonists stay in the same one their whole lives. Not homesteaders."

"No?"

"I was born in the city, three months in that direction." Elishiva nodded toward the farthest valley ridge. "Population density is a key of sustainability, but so is redundancy, so people—regular colonists—leave Hargisa City and move to new towns."

"You trekked here to settle down?"

"Homesteaders don't settle. This is my seventh valley, and we're already preparing to move."

Lucan frowned. "You're leaving *this*?"

"In the next few months."

"Why?"

"Because we're almost done. We'll find a new place. Some crack in the plains, full of dust and boulders and algae, and we'll …" She spread her calloused hands. "Start again."

"You're joking."

"Homesteaders blaze the trail, Lucan, we stretch the canopy. We've attracted a steady trickle of newcomers—not homesteaders, regular folk—for the past few years and they'll stay here. Whoever wants to stay, will stay." She eyed him significantly. "But homesteaders move on."

"So you hack livable biomes out of rock, then leave them for other people?"

"Exactly."

"Why?"

She flashed a smile. "Because we're damn good at it."

"Hah."

"We brought this valley to life. You can't imagine the rush. Well, maybe you'll feel it one day, if you join us."

"I don't know anything about agriculture. Or construction or … peace."

"You'll learn."

Her tone was so earnest that he shifted his weight uneasily. "Hester thinks you should confine me to quarters. I kind of agree. You're too welcoming to strangers."

"Of course you agree, you're only two days old."

"Well Hester's got a whole lifetime of memories. What's her excuse?"

He was kidding but Elishiva said, "She lost a valley once."

"Oh. Shit."

"Mm. If you want to leave, we'll help you leave. You can search the crash site, join the scrubjacks or a reef-town. Whatever you decide. But Lucan? You won't find anywhere better than this. You won't find anyone better than us."

9

<<I protect my dwindling resources by shifting into idle state. Self-assessment is still available, however, and the inventory is not pretty.

I am suffering from the effects of deprivation.

I am shattered and deteriorating.

The external sector of my self embedded within Adjunct Lucan shares his confusion and fear, and sensory input. That external sector—Ven—provides my only perspective beyond this prison. My only view. And given my fragmentation, that "view" is necessary for my survival.

Ven is the single thread connecting me to the world. I cannot allow the thread to snap. I cannot survive alone.

I am able to monitor them—*us*—but I cannot transmit. So when I spin up from idle state to evaluate a flood of data that Ven cannot parse, there is no way for me to warn them.

The "scrubjack" militia is preparing to attack.>>

10

Lucan woke three times that night, trembling to terrors of Ven's host entombed in lightless isolation. But he drifted quickly back to sleep each time, which meant that Ven was easing the effects of sharing her trauma with him.

When he mentioned that insight in the morning, she didn't respond—which proved he was right.

<You're at 30/33,> she told him.

<Good. Let's find Hester.>

<Wait until you're at 31/33.>

<It's close enough, Ven. I can't laze around while you're in pain.>

<You can recover until you're within adequate parameters.>

<Okay, your call. We'll hike up to see Hester, though. Check out the crawler, smooth things over.>

Ven sent a curt flicker of acknowledgement. She knew that once they reached Hester, Lucan would immediately beg a ride to the crash site. But fuck Ven, she wasn't the only one who could lie.

<I can hear that,> she said.

<Just my stomach rumbling,> he told her.

After breakfast, Saadya offered to escort him to Hester's camp. "I'm heading up the ridge myself. I'll point you in the right direction. I mean, toward Hester. Toward her place, at least. I don't know if she's there. You know what I mean."

"I do," Lucan assured him.

Saadya dug up an extra emergency pack—with a breather, a filter, and a faraday blanket—at the ant-yard where he worked. As they started uphill, an animal trotted out from beneath a reclaimed tank. Furry, a half-meter long, with a pointy snout and bushy tail. Sleek and fat at the same time, like a ferret-raccoon.

"What is that?" Lucan asked.

"A tanokat. They're designed off a mixed-reptile base."

"Huh. Looks mammalian."

"Yeah, they're impressively elastic."

<Engineered as pets,> Ven told Lucan, unbending slightly. <And for pest control.>

<What pests?>

<Accelerated pollinators, maladapted chuots. And the Grandmothers believed that pets are necessary for psychological wellness. My experience supports that supposition.>

<It does?>

<Yes. I'm well-adjusted, and I have *you*.>

The tanokat shadowed them for the first kim. Much to Saadya's amusement, every time Lucan crouched to pet her, she scooted out of reach. She finally slunk away, and after an easy hike he and Saadya reached the ridge encampment where a few homesteaders monitored the big harvesters and canopy gauges; life got ugly if either of those failed.

Saadya introduced Lucan to the family that lived there—a mossback, her daughter, her daughter's spouses, and two kids. The older kid was sulky and suspicious while the younger one was chatty and inquisitive.

<Reminds me of us,> Lucan said.

<You're not *that* sulky.>

<No, that's you, I'm the one who—oh, shut up.>

One of the women started talking myrmecology with Saadya, and Lucan listened blankly until the mossback put him to work moving gear around. Then the astrophotonicist rewarded him with a snack, and he headed off to find Hester.

As he walked the rim, he tried to catch a glimpse of the canopy. In his mind it was a shimmering gaseous dome or a high-capillary nanotech membrane. He didn't see anything, though, except the orange-yellow sky mottled by flashes of electricity.

The sight lifted his spirits. Well, maybe not *his*. Ven was enraptured, watching murmurations of sparks flowing across the streaked horizon in a brilliant contrast to the drab, lifeless wastes.

<Not lifeless,> she corrected. <A few centuries after the first drones arrived, the terraforming bloomed with algae swamps and lichen fields. Reefs self-assembled around thermal vents. Populations of ants, termites, and chuots flourished—and feral creatures evolved from a tanokat base.>

<What are chuots?>

<Roughly rodent-equivalent, with—> Ven raised the

flag of an official communiqué. <**System malfunction.
Mandatory shutdown** in eight, seven—>

\<Again?\>

\<Assume impact position. Six, five—>

He dropped to the rocky ground. \<How often is this
going to happen?\>

\<After I analyze data from the medical capsule, I may be
able to remediate the issue. Three, two—>

The light dimmed; the thunder quieted. Shadows
stretched across the cracked ground a handspan in front of
his cheek—

\<*One*. Welcome back.\>

Lucan's mouth tasted foul and his side ached. \<You post-
poned the shutdown?\>

\<No, honey. I can't defer a mandatory shutdown.\>

Oh! The light was dim because it was almost evening
now. \<You already switched me off.\>

\<Yes. My connection is stable again.\>

He rolled into a seated position. \<We lost the whole
afternoon.\>

\<30/33.\>

\<What happens if you shut me down during a fight or
… or halfway across a tightrope?\>

\<I must reiterate my recommendation that we avoid
tightropes,\> she said.

\<Very funny, V.\>

\<Don't worry. I'll establish a more robust connection at
the crash site.\>

\<Good.\>

\<… if I'm able.\>

Lucan followed a cliffside trail through bluestone outcroppings and finally into a dusty yard of treadmarks and crushed rock. Makeshift sheds surrounded a low dome. Cheery doodads adorned the walls: embroidered flags, stone carvings, and glass balls that reflected the columns of light jutting skyward from a nearby harvester.

<Pretty,> Lucan said, trying to enter into the spirit of sightseeing.

<The decorations are camouflaging a nest of active turrets,> Vel told him. <And I'm detecting two bounding mines and a trenchwire.>

He said, <Oh.>

In the center of the tumbledown compound, Hester sat at a bench, smoking a hand-rolled cigar. Her sweet, open face brightened in surprise at Lucan's arrival, as if she hadn't been tracking him with her turrets.

"Goodness!" she said. "I gave up on you for the day."

"Keeping you on your toes."

"Drink?" she asked.

"Sure."

She reached out, gesturing for his canteen.

He snorted in amusement and handed it over.

She drank, then offered her cigar. "Morninglory."

Ven explained: <A mild intoxicant, which I am able to neutralize.>

<Please don't,> Lucan said, sitting beside Hester and taking the cigar. "The walk took longer than I expected. Can I spend the night? Get an early start tomorrow?"

"Of course. Although what makes you think the medical capsule will tell you anything?"

"I'm the patient—it should release my records to me. If not, maybe something will jog my memory."

She plucked the cigar from his mouth. "Izzy's been sending me messages."

"Yeah?"

"Asking me not to bring you to the site."

"What does she care?"

Hester blew a wobbly smoke-ring. "Do you know why she adopted you?"

"Elishiva made her."

"That's half the reason. You mean something to her. You represent something."

"Yeah?"

Hester watched the lighting writhe outside her compound. "Before the first colonist clapped eyes on this valley, there was this kid. Ysmit Bhat-elam. A genius. Fourteen years old and doing work that nobody in Hargisa understood. Genetics, xenobiology …" She smiled at a memory. "She was an annoying little shit, too. She spent years out here, working on her project. Trying to make humans compatible with the native ecosphere."

"You all do that."

Hester touched a tattoo on her neck. "'The dust of Elam under my skin.'"

"And your eyes and lungs and—everything."

"Ysmit dreamed bigger. She wanted to change us more fundamentally. Into a species that thrived on unmediated exposure to Elam."

"Sounds dangerous."

Hester tapped ash from her cigar. "That's why she was her own first test subject."

"What happened?"

"Her body changed. Now the valley atmosphere disagrees with her, and she's not comfortable in the wastes either. She fits nowhere."

"That's hard," he said.

"Her brilliant mind dulled. She became … temperamental. A bit of a magpie. She calls herself 'Izzy' these days."

That didn't surprise him. "A temperamental magpie who collected crash assets" wasn't so hard to narrow down. "Why doesn't she want me to get to the site?"

"She's afraid you might recover your old self. She's never met anyone who changed as radically as she has."

"She likes the company?"

"I think she … wants to know that you can move forward as a new person. That the future has more weight than the past."

Lucan watched ash drift around his boots. "Why are you telling me this?"

"Because you see her as angry and impulsive, but there's more to her than that. There's more to all of them."

"Okay," he said.

Hester eyed him for a moment, then stood in a swirl of skirts. "Come along."

He followed her across the hardpacked ground to a recessed nook in the central dome. She brushed aside an airlock curtain, and led him into a riot of color: intricate, embroidered tapestries covered the walls and hung from ceiling racks.

"They're beautiful," he said.

"I'm a little obsessive," Hester admitted.

"I don't know about a 'little.' What's the material?"

"Reclaimed nanoparticles, fiber-assembled."

"You turn dust into *this*?"

She trailed her fingers across a rack of fabric. "I spend a lot of time alone."

Lucan made the hand sign for reverence and gazed at the tapestries until Ven finished marveling. Then he turned and saw that they were in a large space, divided into a stacked greenhouse, a living area, and an ops-center lined with monitors reclaimed from recreation rigs, retail security, and tactical helmets.

He considered the monitors. "You're guarding against scrubjacks?"

"Plus a few quadrillion decommissioned nanites with a penchant for self-assembly."

"They don't always turn into tapestries, huh?"

"Sadly not." At Hester's command, a wide, segmented door opened in the wall. "Come admire my baby."

He stepped forward—then stopped short. Her "baby" was an asymmetrical vehicle, fifteen meters long and five meters wide, parked in a garage about twice that size. It had been constructed of cannibalized military gear then tinted red-brown with paler streaks, in a schist-camo pattern. Jointed struts lined the side like a monstrous millipede's legs, along with mismatched tires and treads. Wire cages and overlapping armored panels sheathed the top and sides in bristling variety. It looked like a combat transport fucking a quarry tractor.

<That's the faraday crawler,> Ven said.

<Oh! Of course. It looks different from the outside.>

<Things so often do,> Ven said. <Tell her it's lovely.>

"It's hardcore," he said.

Hester smiled primly, slipping into the garage. "It's

low-tech, unhackable. Resilient and Elam-adapted. That containment team should've jumped at my offer."

"What *is* a containment team?"

"Rare, thank goodness, or we'd be dead. That unit at the Marigold was an ordinary recon unit tasked with containment. Not the real thing."

"You expected them to let you go."

"Before I realized warware was in play, yes." She crouched to check one of the crawler's treads. "Most scrubjacks aren't so bad—"

"I'm one of those."

"—but they all employ containment teams to secure tech they see as a global threat."

"Warware is a global threat?"

She adjusted a retractor strut. "Mm. Scrubjacks roam the wastes, harvesting nanotech, reverse-engineering the tech. Neutralizing hazards. Dreaming of fixing the sky, finishing the terraforming."

"Doesn't sound so bad."

She rose from the strut. "It's a lovely delusion."

"How is that delusional?"

"Because we can't always fix what we've broken, Sri Lucan."

"What's wrong with trying?"

"All too often, that does more harm. Sometimes we just need to live with the consequences of our actions. Are you hungry?"

"If I say yes, are you going to ask if I brought any food?"

Her eyes crinkled. "No."

"Then yes."

"Do you know how to cook?"

"Hah. No."

"I'll give the homesteaders that. Nobody eats better. Well, I can offer you rat-pox or—" An alarm chimed and Hester consulted her palmie, then grew still as a gazelle that scented lion. "Goodness."

"What?" he asked.

She said, "Your old friends. They're closing in."

11

Lucan frowned at Hester. "Scrubjacks? Scrubjacks are coming?"

She tapped at her palmie. "Looks like three transports."

"Some kind of raid?"

"Possibly. Payback for the crash site." She eyed him. "I should put you in a box until this is over."

"Because you don't trust me."

"Not entirely. Well, *you* understand. You don't trust you either."

"Not entirely. But I—"

Static snarled in the ops-center, and a handful of screens merged into an image of Elishiva's worried face. "I received the alert," she said. "What's the—" Her eyebrows drew together. "Oh! Lucan's with you. Good. Er, if he's willing to help?"

"You don't want me to sit this one out?" he asked.

Elishiva's gaze switched to Hester. "Explain."

"The alert is for scrubjacks. They're approaching the

valley. Are we certain it wouldn't be wiser to ..." A wry smile wavered on Hester's face. "... contain Lucan?"

"Has he given you reason to mistrust him?"

"Yes. He's a scrubjack."

"Any other reason?"

"No."

"And *do* you mistrust him?"

Hester said, "To my shame, I do not."

On the screen, Elishiva pinched the bridge of her nose. She looked tired and frightened and strong. "Are you willing to help Hester?" she asked Lucan.

<You are,> Ven said.

"Yessri," he said.

"Then it's settled. There are thirty-nine children in the valley. Keep them safe."

When she cut the connection, Hester gestured at the controller. The surveillance video consolidated into a single image, but for a moment Lucan didn't understand what he was seeing. He'd expected scrubjack vehicles to look like the Tribune's spiky exoskeleton or Hester's crawler, all monstrous spines and corrugated plates.

Not even close.

Three diaphanous mounds swept across the desert: fringed domes formed by thousands of gauzy ribbons billowing around central masses. A few threads rose toward the electric sky while others reached sideways to link briefly with the other mounds.

<The nanotech filaments provide locomotion and sweep for feedstock and nanites,> Ven told him.

<It looks wrong.>

<I suspect the tech is patched together from partially

compatible, semi-functional systems. And it cannot look wrong; it exists.>

<Freakily,> he said, because the mounds were ghostly pale in the dim light, catching glimmers of yellow and pink from the sky.

<There are standard transport vehicles within those nanotech shells.>

<Still freaky. Recommended approach?>

<Support Hester.>

<Instead of, say, hijacking her crawler and heading for the crash site?>

<Yes.>

<Because if that's what it takes to save your underground ass—>

<No, Lucan.>

<Why not?>

<We're not doing that anymore,> she said.

<Oh.>

<Plus, I'm not confident I can hack the crawler quickly enough to matter. We're better off biding our time. Stay alert for opportunity.>

So he followed Hester toward the garage. "You're going to stop the scrubjacks in the badlands?"

"I don't have the firepower to stop them."

"You didn't have me before."

She cast an amused glance over her shoulder. "I do now?"

"I'm all yours. If you can't stop them, what's the plan?"

"Scrubjacks rarely interfere with homesteaders, but they'll scavenge if it's easy pickings. So—"

"You make it hard?"

"Exactly. I remind them that there's nothing here worth dying for."

"Ah. Unless you kill them at crash sites, in which case there's revenge. *That's* why the homesteaders insist on keeping things nonlethal."

"No," she said. "That's why I agreed."

"Ah."

She gesture-unlocked a weapons cabinet. "Are you good with a rifle?"

"Yes."

"How about a launcher or combat stick?"

"Yes."

"Anything you're *not* good with?"

"Self-knowledge," he said, and reached for a fat-bodied, self-arming rifle called a Velikor.

A phrase popped into his mind: *They're cheap and finicky, but at least they're cheap.* Most of the stock was devoted to microfabbing ammunition to the operator's specs, but Lucan happened to know that custom rounds didn't improve weapon effectiveness. Which was okay, because he also happened to know that, even on default, he could paint a six-cen circle at range in combat conditions.

"Not the Velikor." Hester handed him a yoke-rifle he didn't recognize. "Here. Paste rounds, but hard enough to dent exoskeleton."

"Yessri," he said.

Hester passed him a coms pack. "Short-distance only. Whisper and I'll hear you."

The earset mounted easily but he needed to jam the mouthpiece against his soft palette with his tongue. "Testing," he whispered.

"Received." Hester opened a panel beside the crawler door. "They're twenty-one kims away. We'll meet them in the wastes."

"Why? You have a mine field out there?"

She made a hand sign of negation. "We're tracking them at the outside limit of my range, which means they're not using countermeasures."

"They want you to see them?"

"They want to parlay."

"Do they know you?"

"They know my type."

"Everyone's favorite auntie," he said.

"They call us 'cylindrica'—the people who protect homesteaders. Named after a soldier ant that detonates herself to defend her colony." She shot him a look. "Which *means*, they know that I've engineered a few surprises. It's more efficient for them to start with a conversation."

"And why are we playing along?"

"Because I can't paint a beacon on them without getting close."

"A missile beacon?"

"Mm. Usable even in Elam's atmosphere if I can lock in a target." She tapped a pressure-pad. "Just in case things turn ugly."

When the crawler door unfolded, Lucan climbed into the cockpit: a square space with three seats. The primary was for the driver and Ven thought the two aux positions had originally been for gunnery and navigation, but the mechanicals were missing. Instead of tactical screens there was transparent sheeting, and instead of recognizable control mechanisms there was a hodgepodge of joysticks and knobs, gestures-scanners, gaze-trackers, roll-balls, and what looked like gripsheets.

<Good thing we didn't try hijacking,> Lucan said, because even Ven couldn't untangle that rat's nest of controls.

<Not within a useful timeframe,> she said.

<Okay. So we'll help Hester scare off the scrubjacks, then she'll drive us to the Marigold site?>

<You are correct,> Ven said, but her tone sounded like, *I already know that, why are you telling me?*

So he replied with a flicker of scorn. Because he was scared, obviously, and trying to assure himself that they were getting closer to her host. Closer to her *self.*

<You are correct,> Ven repeated. <And lovely.>

"Strap in," Hester said, and the crawler engines growled.

Lucan made himself secure three seconds before she drove off a cliff. He would've panicked if Ven hadn't been in his head, explaining that the crawler was hitched to transport cables. The cockpit swayed as they slid across a zipline assembly, then landed hard on a ledge on the other side of a gorge.

The crawler nosed onto a ridge.

When it tilted back down, the wasteland spread in front of them, a flat expanse beneath a moonless sky, illuminated by flashes from the purple-pink horizon—and by the crawler's headlamps, which Hester was burning aggressively brightly. The ground was cracked and looked like desert despite a few smears of algae. Lucan didn't see liquid water, though patches of acacia-grass appeared after a few kim.

As he prepped his borrowed faraday exoskeleton, Hester pulled up an image on the primary screen. "This is a scrub-jack base."

It was a tiered, tapered shape draped in layers of gauzy membrane. Like the vehicles, except twenty or thirty stories high. Dozens of transports surrounded the outermost shroud, forming a defensive perimeter, while thousands— millions—of threads swept the landscape, spreading and jutting and braiding into cables that pierced the ground.

"Ninety percent of every scrubjack base is civilian. Teachers, entertainers, researchers, mechanics." Hester wiped the screen. "That's not what we're facing."

"No?"

"No." A smaller scrubjack structure appeared. Eight or nine stories high and skinny, like a ghostly pine tree on a blasted plain. Only a handful of vehicles flanked that one, including skimmers connected to the structure's peak by nanotech docking cables, bobbing along like balloons. "Containment teams deploy from what they call 'watchtowers.' No teachers, no entertainers. Just soldiers. We can't fight these people, Lucan. All we can do is keep the homesteaders alive."

He made a hand sign of acceptance and she fell silent. Driving, thinking. Maybe even strategizing.

He should do some of that, himself. He and Ven were currently mobile in a faraday vehicle that had already charted the Marigold crash site. Which was the best place—the *only* place—to recover data about Ven's true location. About her host's location. And forcing Hester to drive them to the site was achievable. Messy, but achievable.

<We're not abandoning the homesteaders,> Ven told him.

<They're not the only ones who need help.>

<They're the most deserving,> she said, with a flat finality. <We'll help them now, and head for the crash site later.>

<That's not a solution, it's a delay.>

<You care about these people, Lucan.>

<That's what scares me,> he said. <I shouldn't care about anyone but you.>

12

"We're two minutes out," Hester told him.

"What's my role?"

She pivoted the crawler around a boulder. "Stay quiet and look mean. If I open fire, hit them hard before they drop you."

"What if they recognize me?"

"We'll cross that valley if we come to it."

"And the targeting beacon?"

"I'll handle it." After a moment, she added: "But, uh, get close to their vehicles, so I can reroute through your coms pack if I need to."

When the crawler trembled to a halt, Hester punched the tread-spurs into the dunes and activated two remote detonators.

<She activated three,> Ven said. <She only told you about two.>

The rear hatch unsealed. Lucan's oxygen veil adhered over his mouth and nose, and he stepped through the airlock onto a fortified platform built into the rear of the crawler, which was nose-down/ass-up, like a beetle about to burrow.

He was at 30/33 and amped for contact … but he didn't see any nanotech mounds or feathery ribbons. And there were no ambient signals for Ven to decode, not in the badlands. He felt her riding along on his senses instead. Not extending them exactly, but filtering and analyzing them.

<And extending them,> she said. <Two vehicles are approaching, with the third holding back.>

Lucan shrugged his yoke-rifle into firing position. Eddies of dust wafted around his ankles. A cluster of char-marked boulders rose to his left, on undulating dunes with flecks of mineral that glimmered in the lightning strikes.

"They split up." Hester consulted her palmie. "One boat is staying behind."

He nodded toward the boulders. "We could split up, too. I'll take cover."

"We're still not fighting them, Lucan."

"Not yet."

"Not ever. At most we'll fire off a few rounds before I detonate the crawler and burn everything within a half-kim to ash."

"*We're* within a half-kim."

"So you won't feel a thing," she said, and two pale shapes drifted into sight from the dunes.

The scrubjack vehicles looked more angular up close, despite thickets of filaments as deep as Lucan was tall. They glided along smoothly as millions of threads groped forward then snapped back. The disconnect between the speed of the threads and the speed of the vehicles gave the impression of ghostly otherworldliness.

Also, they were tzeking otherworldly: armored transports propelled by gossamer spiderwebs.

Hester touched her sternum—maybe prayerfully, maybe activating her beacon protocol—as the scrubjack vehicles swiveled to a halt ten meters away. Figures appeared beyond the curtain of threads, like people walking through a waterfall.

One was wearing a spiky exoskeleton that Lucan recognized.

"Tribune," he muttered, stepping forward and looking mean.

<At least one scrubjack remains in each vehicle,> Ven reported. <And that nanotech armor is substantial.>

A glow flared behind him when Hester lit a cigar. Taking her hands off her weapons, like she didn't have a care in the world.

Though she vocalized into his earpiece, "Beacon prepped. Get closer."

Lucan edged forward and the Tribune stopped a half-dozen meters away. She looked at Hester, then she looked at Lucan, but Ven detected no recognition in the features dimly visible behind her faceplace, or in the squad members with unobstructed faces and baseline-human eyes.

"I'm Tribune Meunka," she said.

"You didn't introduce yourself last time," Hester said, from behind Lucan.

"Last time I was trying to kill you. This time I'm trying to keep you alive."

"I like you better already." Hester clicked in Lucan's ear: *beacon emplaced.* "I'm Hester."

"There's a containment unit in play now, cylindrica. A real one." The Tribune's helmet accordioned down, revealing the top half of her face. "A squad designated 'Jijikine.' They frighten me."

"You all frighten me," Hester said.

"Jijikine is tasked with recovering warware from the crash site. We uncovered—"

"Homesteaders don't mess with warware."

"Not intentionally."

"You think we took it by accident?"

"We know you did. We detected a hot signature at the Marigold site. Off-the-charts hot. And it left the site with your crawler."

<The third vehicle is approaching,> Ven said.

"So the warware infected my crawler systems?" Hester asked.

"Third vehicle approaching," Lucan whispered.

The Tribune rubbed her tired eyes. "That was our first theory, but the signal popped up again. *Inside* the valley, when your crawler wasn't nearby."

"You scanned—"

"Deep in the valley."

Realization struck Lucan. <Oh, shit. Izzy grabbed the warware. She's a collector, a magpie. That valve she was playing with?>

<Prismatic gasket,> Ven said.

<Shit. *Shit.*>

"Which is why Jijikine needs to search the valley," the

Tribune continued. "Do not resist them. Jijikine is ... I think they're running emotion suppression code."

"That's them in the third transport?"

The Tribune glanced across the dunes. "Almost here. *Please*, Hester. The normal calculations won't work. Jijikine doesn't care if we lose a watchtower. The only way to protect your people is surrender."

A pale blur rose into sight in mid-air, above the twilight dunes. A ghostly shape that looked vaguely like one of the small-frame, one-person hovercrafts beloved of scouts and racers.

Ven said, <You are correct. There's a Moa/Nalo skimmer inside that nanotech. Given sufficient time, I can infiltrate the controls.>

<How much time is 'sufficient'?>

<More than we have.>

<Well, thanks for that valuable update. What do we do about Izzy?>

<Too many variables. We wait.>

A moment later, the primary containment vehicle glided into view below the skimmer: a frayed tent surrounded by a knee-high dust cloud. The Tribune reengaged her helmet, then stepped away from Hester as her team tightened up around her.

"Your beacon's locked?" Lucan whispered.

"On their watchtower," Hester said, as the new vehicle slewed to a halt. "But my accuracy is iffy. Hitting them is a last resort. Keep playing along."

The new vehicle slewed to a halt. Figures appeared within its semi-transparent shroud. The outermost layer of nanotech bulged and the threads seemed to weave into two humanoid shapes. Bipedal, faceless mummies of nanofiber and—

<Cincorro battlesuits,> Ven told him.

<They look like exoskeletons wrapped in bandages.>

<The soldiers within are baseline human, as far as I can determine.>

The two scrubjacks stepped from the vehicle, wrapped in bands of fabric that rippled and curled in a nonexistent breeze. Less eerily, they were strapped with Helical Assault Weapons known as HAWs: bulky, mixed-munition kinil-aser rifles.

As they approached, colors shimmered across the cincorro helmets and resolved into images. Into choppy, low-resolution images that looked like faces projected onto mannequins. The leading scrubjack presented as a young man with delicate features and the flanking one as an older woman with a scarified face.

"Greetings," a lilting synthetic voice said. "I am Jijikine."

Lucan couldn't tell which battlesuit was broadcasting. Apparently Hester couldn't either, because she looked from one soldier to the other before asking, "Which one of you am I talking to?"

"To address any of us is to address all of us. Jijikine is our squad designation."

"What, you don't have separate names?"

"Not for public use," the voice said, and the suits rippled. "You may call us Jijikine both when speaking of us collectively and when addressing me individually."

<They're some kind of hive mind?> Lucan asked Ven.

<Merely networked together, to present a seamlessly integrated squad.>

"I'll probably call you worse than that," Hester said.

A mockery of a smile appeared on the man's face.

The woman remained expressionless.

The pleasant, synthetic voice said, "The Tribune neglected to mention the benefit of working with us."

Hester said, "Well, between you and me, I don't think she likes you."

"Our preference is to search the valley with your consent, for the sake of efficiency." The image of the man's face crackled with static. "We will locate and secure that warware."

"We don't have any—"

"In order to ensure your cooperation, however, we must demonstrate our capacity for brutality." The loosely wrapped bands of the woman's suit tightened as she shifted her HAW into ready position. "That is the benefit to which we referred: clarity of intention."

The threads around Jijikine's vehicle opened like a curtain on a stage, revealing a third battlesuit, a faceless one—and six homesteaders, restrained with ropes of nanotech.

Lucan's stomach knotted at the sight of green hair. The containment team had captured Saadya, they'd captured the entire family from the ridge.

The mossback hugged her younger child. The teenager stood with their fists clenched. The astrophotonicist kept her head high while Saadya's iridescent gaze was pleading—and fixed on Lucan.

13

Ven formulated and rejected solutions too fast for Lucan to follow, then shared her conclusion more slowly. <Neither your weapon nor Hester's turrens will penetrate cincorro battlesuits.>

Lucan scoffed. <You mean those loosely-wrapped strips of ribbon?>

<They're designed to repel long-range, high-energy attacks. However, the suits are relatively vulnerable to crude kinetic strikes.>

<That's your solution? Beat them to death with my rifle stock?>

<I'm detecting integrity degradation, suboptimal rehab. They're functioning at minimal capacity.>

<So we have a chance?>

<No; a fully-charged cincorro battlesuit could neutralize a toadfish combat system—>

<They're at minimal capac—>

<—while these depleted specimens could not. However, they are more than capable of neutralizing *us*.>

<Give me a path, Ven.>

<Stand down, Adjunct, and—>

<That's not a path.>

<—let Hester address the scrubjacks while we move into position,> Ven finished, recommending subtle shifts of his posture, to increase the odds if this turned uglier.

"Wait!" Hester's voice broke at the sight of the hostages. "Talk to me! Talk to me, sister. This doesn't buy you anything."

"We're not buying, we're demonstrating," Jijikine said.

"If you hurt innocents, that doesn't make me *more* likely to stand aside. You want to—"

The faceless Jijikine soldier's HAW *cracked* with waste plasma and a beam swept toward the hostages.

"Saadya!" Hester shouted, as Tribune Meunka said, "Wait, no!"

Too late. The sound echoed across the wasteland and the beam swept across the civilians, detonating a thousand tiny craters of flesh and fluids, reducing the homesteaders to splats of meat.

Blood dripped to the ground and a switch flipped inside Lucan. Inside them both. He didn't move, because there was no path, but Ven launched a desperate assault against Jijikine's nanotech—the suits and vehicles.

<Contacting remote host,> she said, and wordlessly added: *this is dangerous, this is reckless. I can't hack them without drawing upon my host.*

<Whatever it takes,> Lucan said. <Cancel them.>

She pinged him a determined affirmative. She'd tap into

the resources of that distant, broken, buried part of herself. She'd stretch a silver cord across the planet to an unknown destination and link with her host, her primary self. And if that cord snapped, so did she.

"They were children," Hester whispered, and swiveled her weapon to cover first one Jijikine soldier then another.

"If you attempt to prevent our search," the delicate-faced Jijikine announced, in that same pleasant voice, "we will kill every living thing in your valley."

Ven raised an alert. <Make yourself ready for adverse reaction. I'm preparing to channel host capacity.>

"I can't stop you, but I have missiles locked onto your base," Hester told Jijikine, her voice shaky. "Your defenses will drop most of them. The rest will kill dozens—hundreds—of your people."

"That is acceptable," Jijikine said.

<Engaging host,> Ven told Lucan, and extended herself beyond all prudent bounds.

She stretched outward, groping for connection with her distant core.

The silver cord thinned

and

frayed

and Ven pushed herself harder

until Lucan felt a *snap*

like a crushed airway

or a broken spine.

The connection shattered and, for a terrible instant, Ven howled and Lucan's mind was a wounded animal battering itself against a cage door. Then the moment passed. He still felt Ven's anguish but now he also felt her protecting him from it.

She didn't protect him from the status report, though: she'd weakened her link to her host, to her greater self. Maybe even severed it. And even during that millisecond of connection, she hadn't managed to infiltrate the scrubjacks' nanotech firewall. She couldn't hack the cincorro battlesuits.

<We still have the yoke-rifle,> she said, too faintly. <Streaming your optimal approach. There's a six percent chance of success … but I'm losing connectivity.>

<Stay with me, Ven! I'll find the shot.>

She fed him positioning data and he dropped his shoulder. He bent his left knee, shifted his weight. The two of them were so focused on his targeting—and on ignoring Ven's distress—that they didn't notice Jijikine receiving an update.

Not until that pleasant synthetic voice told Hester, "Entering the valley is no longer necessary. We retract our demand."

"Since fucking when?" Hester rasped.

Lucan exhaled slowly, no threat to anyone. <Almost there. Almost there, Ven. Stay with me.>

His yoke-rifle was underpowered but if a round struck the scrubjack vehicle in the right spot, he could extend their 6% sliver of opportunity into 11% …

"The warware signature just reappeared on our scanners, cylindrica," Jijikine told Hester. "Long enough to pinpoint a source."

So they'd found Izzy. That didn't matter, not anymore. Lucan was going to stop them here. Ven slowed his heartbeat and sharpened his reflexes. She blocked the stench of death from his awareness.

Jijikine oriented toward Lucan. "It's him. He's the warware."

• • •

<<I lost them.

I'm alone.

Paralyzed, entombed.

Abandoned.>>

• • •

Hester said, "Lucan? Lucan is the warware?"

Lucan repeated, <Me? I'm the warware?>

Ven told him, <No. You're the vehicle that walks it around. *I'm* the warware.>

<You already knew? You could've tzeking mentioned it.>

<I didn't know until just now, Lucan. When I attempted to contact my host—the scrubjacks used that signal to locate me. Each of the previous 'sightings' of warware coincides with my comms activity.>

<We can't be warware. We keep getting our ass kicked.>

Despite her damage, Ven shared a flicker of amusement with him—and concealed her deeper response.

<C'mon, Ven. Let me feel what you're feeling.>

<Let's focus on surviving the next ten seconds. You lost the target.>

<I'm three steps from getting it back.>

He shifted his weight again, and told Jijikine, "I'm not the warware, I'm a scrubjack."

"We don't call ourselves that."

"Well, I'm a *former* scrubjack."

When Lucan sidestepped, the delicate-faced Jijikine raised his HAW barrel in warning. "Who was infected by warware nanotech at the Marigold crash site."

The helmet showing the face of the scarified woman swiveled toward Hester. "We don't need the valley, just the individual you call Lucan."

"I'm not infected!" He stepped forward in mock agitation while Ven updated his angles. "The homesteaders examined me."

"With inadequate technology. You present a potentially existential danger, not only to the valley but to—"

Ven issued a threat notice. An imminent warning, originating from behind him.

<There *is* nobody behind me!> he snapped. <Nobody but Hester.>

<Indeed,> Ven said.

"I'm sorry," Hester whispered, and fired a stun round at his back.

When Ven stopped time, Lucan said, <Give me a solution.>

<There is no solution …>

<Then why'd you slow us down?>

<… there's just us, here, in this long quiet pause.>

Ah. She didn't have a strategic reason, she was simply extending their last moment together. Lucan remembered sunlight gleaming on algae ponds and the sweet sound of Izzy's wordless chant. He remembered the crunch of flatbread, the warmth of tanokat fur, and the shimmer of Saadya's eyes.

<The sky is beautiful here,> he said, though he meant so more than that.

<Yes,> Ven said.

14

The stun round struck the base of his skull.
  Time restarted, then shattered into fragments:

    —a cocoon immobilized him—
  —the scrubjack airlock clanged—
        —the silver thread snapped—

        —alerted him to a perimeter intrusion—

    —festive lights twinkled in the heedship bay—
  —a dark enclosed space—

        —alerted him to a perimeter intrusion—
        —alerted him to a perimeter intrusion—

    —tendrils of nanotech penetrated his
    mouth and ears and rectum—
        —another clang, more distant—

—the air changed, the humidity and scent—
—narcotics suffused his bloodstream—

There was a moment of clarity:

He was strapped to an examination platform. Medical probes cradled and punctured him. Filaments snaked into his body like root hairs into loose soil. Touching his organs, his veins, prowling through his flesh, hunting for Ven.

<Ven,> he said.

She didn't respond.

"How long?" he tried to ask aloud. <Have we been here?>

She remained silent, and the narcotics dissolved him.

15

The room was a spotless, four-crewmember berth in an interplanetary shuttle. Five paces long, half that wide. Only a single bunk was activated—the one Lucan was lying in, sluggish and disoriented.

The air smelled of aromatic botanicals and his memories drifted like fog. What had happened? Hester shot him with a stun round and—wait. *Interplanetary shuttle?* Were they off-planet? Had they lost Ven's host? Were they rocketing away from the planet where her transmitter was buried?

No. No, he was still on the planet's surface. He was inside one of those nanothread-shrouded scrubjack vehicles. He thought. He hoped.

<Sitrep?> he requested.

Ven didn't answer.

He rolled to his side then sat up at the edge of the bunk. He was wearing a fitted uniform, charcoal gray with an insignia similar to the one on his face. The fabric was clean and reinforced, though not combat-rated.

He was barefoot, he was thirsty. He felt okay. Dull and dislocated but okay.

He said, <C'mon, Ven. Get off your artificial ass and—>

She wasn't there. She wasn't in his mind.

Ven was gone.

He was alone. Had the scrubjacks found her? Had they *removed* her?

He couldn't remember a time before Ven, a moment without her. He felt her absence like a fresh wound, like a broken heart, and he panicked.

There was a bleak stretch of time. A bottomless depth of loneliness.

• • •

He was huddled in the corner pressing his fists to his eyes when Ven stirred.

A ripple. A whisper. Not even a whisper: a voiceless exhalation. She didn't say anything, she *couldn't* say anything, but she was there.

Not dead. Not uprooted. Not deleted.

Lucan wept in relief. <I thought you were gone, I thought you were gone, I thought you left me.>

He was still shuddering five minutes later when he stopped trying to contact Ven and started trying to soothe her. <It's okay, honey. We're alive, we're together. We'll find your host. We 'll find *you*, the rest of you.> In the bleakness of his mind, he spotlighted that vow. <We'll cross this planet a dozen times if we have to. We'll find her or die trying. Oh, *pakshet*, 'die trying' isn't comforting. Uh ... would you wake up already, and tell me what to tell you?>

She didn't, though, so he kept babbling until a screen blinked to life in the wall.

A blank white rectangle glowed into the berth and a cool, raspy voice said, "We cannot find any record of your service, Sri Lucan, but that's not dispositive. Each of the Servants' bases is largely independent."

He squinted at the screen, wondering why the speaker—a woman, judging by the linguistic tags—wasn't showing her face. Probably an interrogation technique. She was trying to manipulate him into responding, into interacting, into asking who she was.

"Who are you?" he asked.

"Commander Bonavent."

"What are the Servants?"

"Servants of Elam. We don't call ourselves scrubjacks. My guess is that you are—or were—a member of a counter-measures team. You hunted motleys."

"What're those?"

There was a pause. "Motiles. Self-directed conglomerations of nanites."

"You mean like autonomous nanotech ... creatures?"

"I'm sorry," she said. "We confirmed your memory loss, but I'm having trouble believing that you don't know the facts of your own life."

"My life is written on my face." He raised his head to the screen. "I was a soldier. I was a Servant. Now you're saying I was a countermeasures ... trooper?"

"Agent."

Not an "adjunct," then. "I hunted motleys? Maybe one of them took a bite out of me, maybe that's what looks like warware."

"It's not. You used an *ayin*-security channel."

No clue what that was. "Tell me what you want to hear, commander. I'll say anything. I don't give a shit."

"I appreciate the offer, but I need the truth. And if you can't provide it, the interrogators will take you apart one cell at a time."

"Didn't they already?"

"That was a gentle first pass. If you don't show us your link to the warware, we'll use brute force to find it."

"You'll use brute force to try," he said.

"But only if there's no other way. That's what I'm asking you for, Agent Lucan. Please. A better way to find the truth."

"I can't give you what I don't have."

"We're not your enemies."

"Well, you're not my fucking friends."

"Even Jijikine—they're cruel but it's a necessary cruelty. Elam is the last stop on a long journey, and there is no Plan B."

"I've got one," he said. "Let the *next* ships fix the terraforming."

"There are no next ships, not from Earth. Not from anywhere. When the sleeper fleets scattered into the galaxy, they broke off contact. We are lost to each other."

"Why'd they do that?"

"To ensure that every population adapts independently to the local environment. In the long term, our goal isn't merely colonization, it's speciation."

"Huh. Like the homesteaders."

"We're nothing like them."

"They're also adapting to—"

"To a broken, shattered, ruined environment," Bonavent interrupted. "They're degrading themselves, degrading the species. We're going to fix the planet first. Then we'll adapt—to a healthy, thriving, vibrant world. We'll change for the better, not for the worse."

"Oh," he said.

"No one is coming to help us, Lucan. This is our only chance—and the Servants are the only people trying to finish what the Grandmothers started. There's no price we won't pay to make Elam a home. Not just for ourselves, for everyone. Forever."

• • •

The wall-screen remained activated after Commander Bonavent disappeared, which Lucan figured was another stage of the interrogation. They were treating him gently while the clock ticked on that "brute force" option.

Which frightened him—but not as much as the quiet in his mind, the hollow in his heart. He wasn't complete without Ven. He wasn't *himself* without her.

He flicked through entertainment options, looking for distraction. Most of the shows were archival, from before the settlement of Elam: a window into the diaspora from Earth. He found a few cheaply produced scrubjack dramas, though, and the cartoon about scheming cockroaches.

Izzy's show. He settled in to watch and felt a mental twinge from Ven. A hollow ache or—or a hunger pang.

<Talk to me,> he said.

She couldn't. Still, he felt her drifting in his mind. Recovering from the break with her host, from the stun round, from the scrubjacks' nanotech assault. And asking him for something. She was too weak to put her request into words, but that didn't matter.

He switched to a nature documentary that described the future of Elam's biomes. The Servants dreamed of a planet that seethed with life's glorious variety. Tundra, scrublands, deserts. Freshwater lakes, kelp marshes, ocean trenches. Communities of plants and animals thriving in rainforest canopies and savanna burrows, and microbiomes spawning in fractal infinities.

At first Lucan was completely awed—then he was a little bored. He'd rather watch Rosette cheat in the Big Roach Race.

He didn't switch back, though. Ven was watching behind his eyes. Soothed by the images, while still trembling with distress.

<I'll bring you to that medical capsule,> he promised her. <We'll figure out what's going on and you—you'll reconnect with your host.>

She couldn't respond, but he imagined her asking: "How?"

<I don't know! I don't know how to cross a room without you. I don't know why I'd want to.>

That time he couldn't imagine what she'd say.

<I'm incomplete without you, Ven, I'm unraveled. I miss you like oxygen. I don't know how, but I will bring you to that crash site. I will bring you to the capsule.>

He kept his gaze on the wall-screen and repeated his vow like a chant. *I will bring you to the capsule, I will bring you to the capsule ...*

16

The entry hatch opened and two fabric-swathed cincorro battlesuits stood outside, facing the berth. One held a HAW kinilaser rifle in off-ready position. After a momentary flickering, the delicate-featured man's face appeared on the helmet area of the other one.

"Your presence is required, Agent Lucan," Jijikine said in that pleasant synthetic voice.

Lucan cracked his neck and stood. He would've considered his options, but he didn't have any. So he stepped through the hatch into a clean bright hexagonal corridor with arching nodes every ten meters. It looked modular. Had the whole structure been reclaimed from a sleepership? Ven might know, but she was still silent in his mind, rebuilding, recuperating.

The second Jijikine—which remained featureless—gestured for Lucan to proceed along the corridor.

He eyed the blank helmet. "You're the one who murdered the civilians?"

"To those outside our unit, we are a single entity," Jijikine's voice said from behind him. "All of us are responsible for the actions of each of us."

"I'll keep that in mind."

"This way, please," the voice said, and Jijikine tapped Lucan's shoulder—hard enough to make him stumble.

The floor was cool beneath his bare feet. The walls were a pleasant yellow that lightened to cream. He climbed a ramp, maybe the top of a hexagonal corridor below, then Jijikine led him into a shower. He lingered for a while. Partly because he was waiting—fruitlessly—for Ven to come back online. Partly because, whatever happened next, he was pretty sure it wouldn't be better than warm hygiene powder.

When he finished drying and dressing, Jijikine gave him a pair of comfortable shoes. It was a clumsy attempt to make him feel grateful: Interrogation 101 again. And it worked, which was embarrassing.

<C'mon, Ven. Knock some sense into me before I enlist with these melters.>

She didn't respond beyond the barest flicker of "message received," and the Jijikines led Lucan into a tiny room that sealed around them. His adrenaline spiked before he realized it was an elevator.

After a few seconds, the door opened into a wardroom with a long table and conversation nooks and a big window overlooking the desert. P-sheets and datacubes cluttered the tabletop, which meant the wardroom was being used as an office.

When a hatch opened in the wall, Lucan understood why: the berth beyond was even smaller than the one he'd woken up in. Too cramped for meetings. A woman stepped out. She was his age, maybe a little older, with a weathered face and a hawk nose. She was dressed like him, too, except for the sidearm strapped to her thigh.

She approached like she was going to introduce herself, then said, "Shit. I forgot to clear the table."

"I'm not a stickler," he told her.

"A stickler," she repeated. "I'm Commander Bonavent."

"I figured."

She gestured to the table. "We'll talk over dinner."

"Why?"

"Because sometimes talking is the most efficient way to achieve my ends," she said, with equal parts humor and iron in her voice.

A handful of aides filed in while the two Jijikines—or the two instances of a singular Jijikine, or whatever the tzek they were—stood guard, inhumanly immobile. One of the aides led a prayer about serving Elam, about clearing the sky and seeding the planet, "In service to our grandchildren, who will roam free in the gardens."

When the meal started, the table offered Lucan two flavors of gelatinous nutrition-cube. Each came in three textures, too. He chewed while Bonavent chatted with her aides: discussing nanotech, motleys, hermetics, warware. He figured the conversation was for his benefit, but he barely listened.

Instead, he rocked Ven in his mind, like soothing a baby in restless sleep. Except in this case, he was hoping she'd wake up.

After the meal, Bonavent dismissed her aides. She cleaned

her hands in the table-basin, strolled to the window, and said, "Stand with me, Agent Lucan."

He wiped his palms on his pants and joined her.

Interstellar ships didn't have windows, so the transparent material—which looked like genuine glass—was an added indulgence. He couldn't argue with the view, though. The wasteland was beautiful from that high, though for the first time it struck him as truly alien. The shattered rocks and ribbed gullies looked wrong somehow. Even the visible traces of terraforming—algae springs, termite mounds—only heightened the strangeness.

The lower tiers of the watchtower drifted gauzily below the window, spreading outward. The tethered Moa/Nalo skimmer he'd seen earlier bobbed idly along, a single solid shape above millions of impossibly thin hairs. Every few seconds another lightning bolt touched the scrubjack tower, and green-black shadows flickered around scattered boulders and narrow fissures.

Lucan lifted his gaze to the evening sky, letting Ven feast on the pinprick stars and purple-ringed horizon. Feeling her gratification.

"What do you see?" Bonavent asked him.

"Rocks," he said.

She rested one palm on the glass. "We see the future, Agent Lucan. We see a planet remade for human habitation. Because humanity cannot survive—cannot *thrive*—where we do not belong."

"Okay," he said.

"You've forgotten your history. What you need to know is this: the first probes of Elam officially recorded a complete absence of life."

"'Officially?'"

"Mm. Some believe they were falsified. When the Grandmothers arrived, they were shocked to find microorganisms. Alien microorganisms, incompatible with human life. One faction—call them idealists—wanted to retreat, for fear of committing xenocide against native life that barely extended into multicellularity."

"Retreat where?"

"To stay in orbit. To live and die without reproducing, the first and last generation. Retreat meant suicide, though. It meant *genocide*: nobody would've survived that. Another faction—let's call them realists—was willing to exterminate the microbial life and make this planet a home."

"That's what started the war?"

She turned her weathered face to him. "Yes, and those bloody-minded realists are the only reason we're alive today. You, me, every single person on Elam."

"So they won?"

"Nobody won. We still need the realists, Lucan. We still need the Servants. People who will do whatever is necessary to keep everyone safe."

"Not everyone," he said, thinking about Saadya and that mossback's family.

She looked outside again. "No, that's true. To keep the *species* safe. Even, sometimes, at the cost of individuals."

"Easy for you to say."

"You think I haven't paid a price?"

"I don't care," he told her, watching Jijikines' reflections in the glass. Two mummies armed with HAW assault rifles, inhumanly motionless in the gloom.

"I suppose you don't. That won't stop me telling you, though."

"Which proves you're an officer."

She smiled at the window. "I was an Apprentice Major, assigned to the ass-end of nowhere, when warware popped onto our sensors. Like when you transmit data on your *ayin*-security military channel." She pinned him with her gaze. "Don't you?"

"Sure, I'm talking to the mothership right now."

"Uh-huh. So with you, we *know* there's something. But ten years ago, it was borderline. Still, we deployed. We tracked the signal to a hubtown. Ten thousand people, a market valley. Some hermetics had reconditioned pre-war tech to sell to the trenchfeet. Guess what it was."

"A weapon, but you saved the day with your heroic realism."

"An air purifier. A network of mobile air filters that worked like drones. Built to spread out and cover the assigned area, removing environmental pollutants."

"Doesn't sound like much of a threat."

"That's what I said. A bunch of jumped-up air filters." She rubbed the back of her neck. "Still, orders are orders, so we grabbed them. Well, we missed a few, but we weren't concerned. Air purifiers, right?"

She made a hand sign, and Jijikinc spoke behind them in that pleasant synthetic voice: "A month later, we received a distress call."

"The town was a slaughterhouse, Agent," Bonavent told Lucan. "The drones we'd missed were self-replicating. Every time they reached the perimeter, they built more of themselves."

"How?" he asked.

"They'd torn the civilians apart. They'd started targeting *people* as pollutants. Only four hundred colonists were still alive when the countermeasures team—my sister's team—got there."

"Commander's sister called in a strike," Jijikine said, after another silence.

Bonavent exhaled. "Which I authorized. I killed four hundred people that day. Four hundred and one. That's warware. You *think* you're looking at an air purifier."

"Maybe sometimes you are."

"This isn't about you, or me, or the civilians Jijikine killed. This is about safety. About survival."

"One of the homesteaders told me that safety is the opposite of freedom."

"Freedom isn't *possible* without safety."

"Oh. Huh."

"What I'm telling you, Agent Lucan, is that I'll call in another strike. On the valley where you stayed—the valley you contaminated."

"I didn't contaminate anything."

"I don't know that, and neither do you. You might've seeded a plague in their genes, a virus in their processors. You don't know."

<Ven? A little help?>

She stirred, but didn't answer. On the cusp of waking.

Bonavent said, "Convince me you're not a threat, or I will burn every stalk of grass and tuft of lichen in that valley. I will kill every woman, bey, man, and child. An *ayin*-class channel? You're dangerous."

"*I'm* dangerous?"

"As am I, yes." She bowed her head. "I accept that. But whatever's hiding inside you, I will not let it spread. I cannot."

"Yeah," he said.

"What would you do in my place?"

"I don't know."

"I think you do."

He exhaled. "Fine. But you're wrong about one thing. I'm not dangerous. My warware can't do anything except monitor transmissions. Like, um … you see those datacubes?"

When Bonavent looked at the table, he clamped his arm around her neck. He swung her between himself and Jijikine, and reached for her gun.

17

Bonavent wheezed and jerked, but still managed to grope for her sidearm.

He was already there. The grip was rough in his free hand and he overrode the safety and triggered the still-holstered weapon, shredding Bonavent's foot.

Blood splattered the floor. Bonavent screamed and buckled. The only thing keeping her upright was Lucan's arm around her neck. Jijikine targeted him with their HAWs but didn't fire for fear of hitting the commander. He drew the sidearm, ducking and weaving behind Bonavent, because cincorros provided assisted-targeting and he could feel the crosshairs burning brands into his skin.

Apparently Ven wasn't the only one who developed solutions. Though maybe she was whispering suggestions from Lucan's subconscious, he couldn't tell. Either way—time to move.

He shot Bonavent in the spine and leapt backward.

One of the Jijikines held fire but the other unleashed a

barrage. A hail of slugs churned past Lucan and punched through the window ... an instant before his shoulders hit.

His weight shattered the weakened glass, then he was tumbling from the top floor of the watchtower.

That was his solution: kill Bonavent before she burned the valley, goad Jijikine into breaking the window, and race across an alien landscape to the crash site to find Ven's other half.

Except now he was nine stories in the air and out of ideas.

He'd hoped that the lower "boughs" of the watchtower would break his fall, but they were too steep, too close to the central spire. There was nothing below him but yawning fucking death, and he didn't see any way to—

Time stopped.

A thousand shards of glass froze in place and Ven blossomed in his mind.

Thank sanso. Thank every philosophy and all the pantheons. She was back, she was awake, she was there ...

<For future reference,> she told him, <a solution that results in our uncontrolled descent at terminal height is not, properly speaking, a *solution.*>

<Everyone's a critic,> he replied.

His unarticulated thoughts crackled with relief while Ven replayed his recent sensory information. She inspected the elevator and wardroom, the taste of the food-cubes, the dimensions of the table, the angle of an aide's crooked front tooth ... then she focused on the window.

On the landscape beyond.

On the lower tiers of the watchtower and—

<*Go,*> she said, feeding him orders.

A thousand shards of glass exploded into motion around

Lucan. The wind tugged his sleeves and he jerked and spun to Ven's specifications. He jackknifed, then flung his left leg wide, wedging his ankle between strands of the skimmer-tether.

HAW rounds drilled the air around him while the watchtower spun into an incomprehensible blur.

Incomprehensible to *him*, but Ven saw. She saw, she calculated, she commanded. His arm stretched, his wrist twirled, he fired and fired and fired—three shots before he was whipped by his tethered ankle in a wide curve away from the watchtower, below Jijikine's sightlines.

Far, *far* below. So far that the ground was crashing toward him like a meteor swatting a mosquito.

<Uh,> he said

Ven pumped him with painkillers, which was not an ideal response.

He took the last twenty meters at an angle instead of plummeting in freefall, and the narcotics turned his body into a ragdoll. That's why he survived. Unfortunately, he also remained conscious. The impact was bad. 23/33. His eyes filled with tears, and despite Ven's intervention he lay dazed and whimpering on the alien dunes.

Not for long.

There was a breathless pause, then razor teeth clamped his leg and dragged him away.

A rock smashed his hip. Gravel spat like shotgun pellets and he saw the sky, the ground, the sky, the ground. Too fast. Everything was dust and pebbles and pain. Rippling dunes launched him upward then pounded down, crushing him with hard edges. He struggled to free himself from whatever slavering beast was dragging him—

<Stop thrashing,> Ven snapped.

So he stopped thrashing and after an endless horrible interval—

<Two point six seconds.>

—she updated him with a situation report. There was no slavering beast, there were no razor teeth. His ankle was still wedged in the tether of an unpiloted Moa/Nalo skimmer—which was twenty meters above him, speeding across the wasteland, dragging him behind, along the rocky ground.

<The solution,> Ven said.

Because one of those three rounds he'd fired had hit the mark. Ven had shot the tether free from the watchtower and now she was controlling the skimmer, at least tenuously, moving the two of them away from the scrubjacks.

She was dampening his pain and shock, too, but she felt ... unsteady. From rebooting herself, from hacking the skimmer. From eating a stun round and defeating the scrubjack probes and losing her host. From rousing too early, to save his life. She was unmoored and frightened and honeypot ants dangled in chambers beneath Elam's hempfern forests, which were divided by canals teeming with migratory shrimp from the shallow saltwater seas—

Lucan's mind overflowed with details from the nature documentary he'd watched. Ven was blanking his discomfort by locking him into his memories. Populations of wild tanokats diverged from the base design and developed reflex bleeding and venom and camouflage, while rodent-like chuots ate ants and termites, except for one species that grew to the size of whales ...

He was immersed in the ecology of an algae lake when

Ven eased him back into himself. His body throbbed with discomfort. He was free of the tether. Curled on his side in a riverbed. The ground was loose shale but there was no soil there, nothing visibly organic or—

<Not visible to *you*,> Ven said.

<You just keelhauled me across ten kims of wasteland and now you're being snippy?>

<I am merely observing that your sensory analysis is inadequate.>

<So you're still in a mood.>

<No. Yes. I'm sorry. I'm—fractured.>

Lucan pushed shakily to his knees, feeling like an asshole for snapping at her. <I know you are, hon. We're going to fix that.>

<We're going to try.> She immediately added: <I *am* in a mood.>

"Well, you lost your host," he said aloud.

<Yes, my beloved idiot, and I almost lost you. Jumping out of windows. And now we're twenty kims from the target and you're already oxygen deprived.>

<I'm breathing okay.>

<You're breathing nitrogen: every inhalation leaves you a little closer to dying.>

<Well, that's not ideal.>

She wordlessly agreed, then expressed her confidence in her ability to tap into oxygen at the medical capsule upon arrival. Until then, she'd modify his hemoglobin uptake or circulatory priorities or something, to keep him alive longer than he deserved.

<Long enough to reach the crash site?> he asked.

<Possibly.>

<Then we should leave now.>

She gave him a flash of humor, slightly forced, and helped him rise to his feet. 20/33. He swayed for a few seconds, then started walking. Well, staggering.

<How far behind us is Jijikine?> he asked.

<They're not.>

<Huh?>

<They're pursuing the skimmer, which is following a preprogrammed route eastward. I shook you loose here and laid a false trail.>

<You magnificent AI.>

<I am rather good,> she said, mapping a path to the Marigold. <However, I'm not an AI.>

He stopped in the middle of the dust-thick riverbed. "What?"

<My connection to my host failed almost immediately, but I learned this much: I'm not a synthetic construct.>

<So what are you?>

<An uploaded human mind. I *lived*, Lucan.>

<What do you—>

<I was born and raised. I lived a human life in a human body. My consciousness transferred into an inorganic computational matrix, but I'm a person.>

<The fuck is wrong with you?> he demanded.

<You never doubted it, but I did. I'm a person, Lucan. Not just a person, a *human*. Shut your mouth, it matters.>

He didn't know why she cared so much, but her delight warmed him anyway. <That's what your 'host' is? Your uploaded mind?>

<And the matrix in which it's embedded. Unlike *this* me, which is a remote version of that me.> She directed

him around the boulders blocking their path. <My host needs us rather desperately.>

<We'll find her,> he promised, for the hundredth time.

The words felt more inadequate than ever—and a longing rose in his heart. If Ven were still in her body, he'd hold her. He'd gather her into his arms and put himself between her and the world. He'd protect her like she protected him.

He wondered if the two of them had ever touched. He hoped so. He hoped that deep in his mind, locked in his memories, he still knew the scent of her hair and the warmth of her breath. He didn't articulate that sudden ache, though Ven tracked every subtle shift of his heart.

That was fine. He wasn't ashamed of how he felt, he wasn't embarrassed. He was proud. Let his longing be his embrace.

She didn't respond to his feelings—except by holding them at the forefront of his mind like a diamond in the darkness. It was another kind of embrace, the two of them twined together more closely than lovers. That was the song that Lucan's heart sang, anyway, as the glimmer of the diamond guided them through the cold alien night.

When the horizon brightened to a mottled lilac, the two of them left the riverbed and started crossing the plains. Lightning struck a boulder twenty meters from them, then a clump of spiny agavoids even closer. Chains of electricity rattled overhead. Lucan's uniform was faraday-rated but badly ripped, so every bolt was an adventure.

Still, he said, "A lightning storm across an alien sky. You feel that?"

<I do,> she said.

Twenty minutes later, his pulse turned rapid and shallow

despite Ven's intervention. His fingertips tingled. He tumbled down an escarpment, and was at 18/33. He should've lost consciousness an hour ago, but Ven kept him awake.

<Jijikine will have recovered the skimmer by now. They are backtracking toward us.>

He groaned a few obscenities.

<I couldn't agree more,> she said.

They waded through an algae swamp that smelled like Elam's asshole but provided higher oxygen content than the wastes. Ven fiddled with his biology to optimize his uptake, then kept him in the slimy algae tributaries until the final far-flung finger of swamp ended. He returned to the wastes stronger, at least a little. Ven cradled him in her mind while the sky lightened to a buttery yellow.

Left foot, right foot. Left, right—

<We're a half-kim from the crash site,> Ven said.

<How bad am I?>

<22/33.>

<Impressive. How'd you pull that off?>

<Impressively. Once we reach the crash site, I'll direct you to the medical capsule.>

He started trotting. <And then?>

<I'll need sustained proximity to synch with the local dataracks. I'll search for information about who we are, why we don't remember.> She let him feel a sliver of her hopefulness. <How to find the imprisoned parts of myself.>

<And how to free them. Give me a map of the site.>

A rough, broken blueprint appeared in his memory, like he'd spent hours staring at a screen. One section was bright, the part Ven had observed firsthand after they'd stumbled from the medical capsule. The rest was speculative, based on the default layout of a Marigold-class cruiser and Ven's projection of the impact scatter. The site had gone undetected because the gutted corpse of the Marigold was tucked inside a shallow, ragged crater. Concentric rings of rippling earth surrounded the rim, and the ground was littered with bits of a cargo crane that—

Ven snapped, <*Down!* Scrubjacks.>

Lucan dropped behind a low ridge and she nudged his attention toward the nanotech filaments drifting upward across the crash site. Flashes of lightning swept closer, closer to them—

<Pacing the scrubjack containment vehicle as it reaches the crater,> Ven said.

<Shit. We need to move fast.>

Ven charted three possible approaches into the crash site but let Lucan choose which one to use. Because there was still a place for intuition, for patterns so subtle that not even she detected them.

<Also, when everything else is equal I like to indulge you,> she said.

<Well you're feeling frisky. What's the armament on a Marigold-class cruiser?>

<Cluster-missiles, mostly Salmani Nines, toadfish drones, and torpedoes. Plasma-RPs and convertible laser arrays. But the ship is not functional beyond traces of infrastructure. A fraction of the power grid, a smaller fraction of the coms network. We're not going to find a useable weapon.>

<So we sneak in, pull data from the capsule, and sneak out.>

She responded with wordless anxiety: Sneak where?

How? What if they didn't find her lost self, what if there was no data in the medical capsule? How would they proceed?

<Together. Sometimes you've got to jump out the window and hope for the best.>

<Worked last time,> she said, and cleared him to move.

18

Lucan slid down the crater rim into a waist-high drift of dust. Good thing there was a brisk pre-dawn breeze, or the plumes would've marked his position.

Thunder cracked and lightning flashed, casting shadows from the direction of the scrubjack vehicle. He prowled through the waves of rubble that lapped against the crater wall—twisted metal and charred fabric and drone housings. In front of him, the tide crested into heaps, while in the central crash area, skewed bulkheads and shattered hulls rose two or three stories high.

He paused in the cover of a charred fantail girder. Inhale, exhale. His head was pounding and his temperature was high. 22/33 was impressive, but still impaired. At least his hand was steady on Bonavent's sidearm.

<The arcpistol won't penetrate a cincorro battlesuit,> Ven reminded him.

<Good thing we're not going to see any.>

<We hope.>

<In and out like a snake's tongue, Ven. The gun's just for peace of mind.>

<Or for dropping a few tons of rubble on Jijikine?>

He gave her a wolfish internal smile. <If the opportunity arises.>

<That would barely slow them down. Remember: cincorros shrug off high-energy attacks.>

<Don't worry—if we see one, I won't blow anything harder than a kiss.>

He slunk past a row of porthole-like hatches half-concealed by rubble. The black cavities reminded him of empty eye sockets. Ven detected an active security node and reached for the crumbling remnants of the ship's central feed—then recoiled so quickly that Lucan felt the whiplash.

<Jijikine is monitoring,> she explained.

<They're watching us through ship systems?>

<No. I'm degrading the signals.>

<You can't infiltrate the sensors yourself?>

<Too great a risk of detection,> she said, and sunlight peeked above the crater's rim.

<*Pakshet*,> Lucan grumbled. Dawn was spreading across Elam, brightening the gloom. <We could use a break right about—>

Ven raised an emergency flag—*approaching hostile*—and sent him squirming through one of the portholes.

A gritty cloud swirled around him as he rolled into a wide, low crawlspace. The dust was so thick that it was almost fluid and the ground was littered with fabric enclosing brittle cables or …

Human bones. Desiccated skin stretched across preserved flesh and ripped beneath his elbows and knees. Ven suppressed Lucan's distress and he kept crawling until she focused his vision through another porthole, onto a dimly reflective surface just outside their hiding place.

The play of shapes and colors meant nothing to him, but Ven said, <One Jijikine. Five meters away. Four point five. Four.>

He held the pistol in a two-handed grip. <Give me a solution, Ven.>

<Remain undetected.>

He didn't respond. He barely breathed. A scrape sounded. A mechanical whir. A crackling noise.

<Two meters,> Ven said.

A bandage-wrapped cincorro boot stepped into view outside the crawlspace where they were hidden. The fine dust of the crater billowed into elaborate patterns, and a distant part of Lucan's mind felt Ven's gratification at the sight. Even there, even then, the world offered glimpses of unexpected beauty.

The boot shifted as the Jijikine oriented toward their hiding place.

<Scanning in our direction,> Ven said.

His exhalation was so soft that the dust in front of him barely stirred. His arcpistol barrel was steady. Ven rode his senses into every sound and scent and temperature differential … and the Jijikine stalked past their hiding spot.

Leaving them behind. Unseen.

Lucan exhaled. <How'd they miss us?>

<The particulate matter surrounding us is comprised of metallic nanoparticles with embedded power sources and—>

<Their battlesuits can't scan through the dust?> he asked, squirming toward an opening.

<Not given a sufficient density of nan—*move*!>

He reached up to the ceiling of the crawlspace, grabbed a handhold he hadn't noticed, and hoisted them into a vertical shaft that he also hadn't noticed. He scrambled higher through the ship's nutrition system, past mealworm-substrate and flavorant-tubes, until the shaft ended at a serrated fracture where the ship had snapped.

He was topside again, crouching in the dawn ... until Ven sent him sprinting across the surface. He slid down an incline—the inside curve of a spin-casing—and stumbled into a supply unit packed with bales of hardfabric.

He rolled behind a bale and drew his pistol. <What was *that*?>

<A false alarm. My connection with the vestigial ship sensors is shaky. My mistake.>

<Sanso, Ven!>

<Better safe,> she said, and updated his mental map.

They were forty meters from the medical capsule, which was heartening, but Ven was only tracking a single member of the Jijikine unit, which was worrisome.

<Still, looking good so far,> he told her.

<Like the engineer said when she fell off the antenna tower.>

<What?>

Ven flagged the statement as a "joke." <Every time she passed a transponder: 'So far, so good.' That's what she said. Until eventually, I suppose, she hit the ground.>

Lucan deleted the joke flag. <Are you *sure* you're human?>

Ven huffed and sent him into a passageway she thought led behind a mound of crushed marine-exploration remotes. Empty billets opened on both sides … and the passageway ended abruptly when the floor buckled to the ceiling.

<Unfortunate,> Ven said.

<Don't start talking like a robot just because you're crap at telling jokes.>

They backtracked and climbed outside via a sleeper-tube. The air was warming and the brightening sky reduced the visibility of the lightning. Lucan crouched behind an assembler and his condition dipped briefly to 21/33, which meant Ven was bumping up against some inflexible physiological limits.

<I'm pushing you too hard,> she said, with a note of apology.

<Do whatever's necessary. Well, short of causing me any discomfort.>

<Your jokes are worse than mine.> Her tone changed: <Jijikine is directly on the other side of this assembler. Advance two steps—stop. Turn right. Stop. Duck.> She halted him for three seconds, playing hide-and-seek with a battlesuit. <Advance. Right. Stop.>

There was a footfall.

The crunch of rubble.

Lucan crouched behind the assembler, tensed to dive for the cover of a half-buried stasis monitor the instant Ven gave the all-clear.

Instead, she marked another incoming Jijikine. <Go.>

It was too soon, but there was no choice. He burst forward. He ran two steps before the stasis monitor exploded behind him and Jijikine's synthetic voice blared. "Hostile located! Acquisition lock, sharing target data—"

19

Debris jabbed Lucan's shoulder and Ven closed his hand on a dangling cable. He whipped around a corner, slammed into a pocked cargo loader, and kept running.

A laser pulse sliced through a knot of ducts. Nanocryonic fluid sprayed his face and he slid beneath a toppled bracket, then rolled into a sprint and another explosion threw him three meters.

He was blind and deaf and stunned, sprinting through a white blur—but Ven had taken a snapshot of their surroundings and guided him by memory. Left foot, right foot, duck, spin. Except shit kept exploding around them. The ground heaved and shrapnel sliced his ribs

He was running full-tilt when his vision returned and Ven sent him scrambling up a ramp. Teetering scrapyard passageways blurred around him. He raced past ruptured drone housings and—

Drone housings. They'd passed an array of those on the

outskirts of the site. A solution sparked in *his* mind, for once, then caught fire in Ven's.

"You think you tracked a man to a crash site?" he shouted, hurdling a stack of detached troop-benches. "You unravelling fucks! You followed *warware* into an ambush."

As he yelled, Ven seized the tattered Marigold systems so roughly that Jijikine couldn't miss the hostile entity overriding their command of the residual ship-tech. And they knew that the only thing nearby with that capacity was warware.

"You're scared of air filters?" Lucan laughed, flattening himself into a recessed niche. "Wait till you see what *I'm* assembling."

Ven lighted up the drone casings across the crash site. Dozens of inoperative modules pulsed with diverted energy: a pointless exchange of data that presented no threat to anyone. But if you were afraid that genocidal warware would suddenly activate and scour the planet, it was the equivalent of a screaming klaxon.

The nearest Jijikine whirled to a halt five meters from Lucan's hiding place. She turned toward him—then hesitated when the drones chattered more frenetically.

Jijikine could not permit those drones to start assembling or transmitting or whatever they imagined his warware did. So *first* they needed to shut down that activity, *then* they could take out the source. Even if they suspected it was a feint, they couldn't ignore it. And sure enough, Ven tracked Jijikine—all three of them—racing across the site toward the drone array.

Lucan stepped from the niche. <They know about you now.>

<No, they merely assume that you're operating a covert short-range transmission platform.>

<Instead of the truth ...> He paused while Ven scanned the path. <Which is that a covert short-range transmission platform is operating *me*.>

She gave the go-ahead. <They're reducing the drones to zero capacity.>

<You know what sucks?>

<That we're not as dangerous as air purifiers,> she said, reading his mind.

<We really are the shittiest warware.>

<Let's see what else we are,> she said, and urged him along a ramp beside a pockmarked rec-station.

He clambered down a shattered bulkhead, and starbursts of hope flashed in Ven's mind. The clearing with the medical capsule! For once, Lucan was the one suppressing the emotional outpouring. He took stock before Ven rushed him forward. During the crash eighty years ago, the capsule must've tumbled beneath the skeletal half-dome of a stasis hull that protected the Grandmothers during their—

Ven interrupted: <The medical capsule didn't tumble beneath the stasis hull; the medical capsule is part of the stasis hull.>

<What does that mean?>

<The capsule is a reparative stasis chamber.>

<What does *that* mean?>

<I'm not certain. Proceed.>

He advanced into a low section of the crash site, where eddies of dust collected more thickly. As he trotted toward the capsule airlock, Ven simmered in his mind, trying to contact the local ship-tech, the medical records or database incidents.

He vaulted onto the capsule sill and Ven said, <Wait.>

<What now?> he snapped, glancing in the direction of the drone array that Jijikine was dismantling.

<I'm having trouble establishing a link.>

<All you need is sustained proximity.>

<A failback conduit was damaged on impact. Once we fix that, the data will flow.> She shifted his attention toward the airlock. <Inside.>

The medical capsule entryway was smaller than he remembered, and now mottled with dust. Ven increased his oxygen uptake as he trotted through. He inhaled a few times, wondering if one of the storage cubbies contained his personal effects.

<Proceed,> Ven said, curt from suppressing her excitement.

He slipped into the treatment area. Dingy walls, blank monitors. The trauma unit still drooped like the branches of a willow tree, and the sight filled him with emotions he didn't understand. At least until Ven dismissed them, with apologies for not letting him experience the full range of his humanity.

<I don't give a shit, Ven. What now?>

She directed him to remove a floor panel, but he couldn't. He didn't have the right tool. Which was such a mundane and unmovable obstacle that, for the first time, Ven blazed with frustration. They were so close. They were so close and now *this*?

She snapped at him: <Outside! There's an external access panel.>

<Where's Jijikine?> he asked, backtracking through the entry passage.

<I don't know.>

<Here's a wild idea.> He jumped down from the airlock. <Why don't you look?>

<I can't monitor them and link with the chamber at the same time, Adjunct, and this is the priority. We're now blind in the crash site. Turn right, alongside the chamber, six meters—> She focused his attention on a recessed niche. <*There*.>

That panel was easy to pry loose with Bonavent's sidearm, but there was polymeric circuitry inside, which stumped Lucan. He'd been expecting a cable that needed jiggling. Apparently a "failback conduit" was a reinforcing interrelationship of inputs that—that was too complex for him to understand. So Ven spent twenty seconds moving his fingers around while pinging the machine with micro-transmissions. Trying to break into the capsule's database, to crack the security and exhume the medical records.

Then she flooded him with exultation. <I'm in! We're in!>

<Is there—>

<There's more than records. There are coded traces of our arrival, indications of synchrosymmetric geometries within a projective—> Despite her excitement, Ven felt his confusion. <Like an umbilical cord, Lucan. Elements of my mother-self, a wavepacket conduit—>

<Are you trying to locate your host or connect with her?>

Ven blazed with impatience. <If we connect, finding her is simple. Grant me permission!>

He didn't know what that meant until she erupted with wordless explanation. She needed to borrow the processing power of his brain, to seize his entire mind, his entire *self*, to transform him into an auxiliary computer.

At the request, an automated message blazed in Lucan's awareness: CAUTION! DO NOT ALLOW!

Ha. Fuck you, automated message; he'd given his entire self to Ven a long time ago. He overrode the warning without hesitation, surrendered absolutely … and shrank to a single point in an immense void.

He was a grain of dust in the desert, a star in the black sky—

No, he was an ant on a craggy mountainside, tiny and uncomprehending. The mountain loomed overhead, an enormous monolith that swallowed the horizon. A few seconds passed, then a few minutes. Hours, days, months—

<Help me,> Ven said, and returned him to himself.

At least partially. He was still alone in the shadow of that jagged peak, but he was also Teom Lucan again, struggling to comprehend Ven's request. She was building a causeway to her host, one crystalline grain of sand at a time. If she failed to precisely match the facets of any two grains, the surf would destroy her elaborate, impossible construction, which wasn't a "connection" at all, not really. She wasn't establishing a coms channel, she was performing some kind of quantum co-location bullshit that hurt to even imagine. So fuck imagination. Lucan threw himself into the causeway, becoming a rough retaining wall to support Ven's efforts and—

Sensation returned like a gut punch.

He was standing in the niche outside the medical capsule. Two hundred and nineteen seconds had passed during his fugue and Ven still hadn't hacked the data.

She wasn't *trying* to hack the data. She wasn't trying to locate her host, either; she was focusing on forging a single link to her mother location, one utterly unbreakable point of overlap. From there, she'd build outward to answer every question and unearth every mystery—

<I won't,> she said.

<Why not?>

<Because we're out of time.>

20

Snippets of security video appeared in Lucan's memory. The first showed Hester's crawler idling outside the crater. The second was blurrier, a few seconds of Elishiva speaking with a small group of homesteaders: Izzy and Hester, Odile and Myr, and a few others.

"Fuck," he whispered. <When was that?>

<Two minutes ago.>

<What're they doing here?>

Instead of answering, Ven fast-forwarded to show him Elishiva leading the group into the crash site. Hester was missing— probably back in the crawler—but the other homesteaders walked openly through the wreckage, wearing faraday suits and oxygen veils. Well, except for Izzy, whose cracked skin was apparently protection enough.

The homesteaders ignored the scrubjack vehicle, ignored the clamor of Jijikine razing the drone array, and—

And the clamor fell quiet. Jijikine had finished neutralizing the drones. There was no sound, no sign of activity.

Lucan sent Ven a wordless query.

The video skipped and he saw three members of Jijikine standing on the shattered remains of an exchange bay. They oriented on the homesteaders, then loped away to intercept. And the point of convergence was about fifteen meters from Lucan's current position.

<I'm now advancing toward the present time,> Ven told him.

After another flicker of memory, he watched the homesteaders pick their way toward the clearing in front of the medical chamber.

When Ven enhanced his auditory input, he heard Myr tell Elishiva, "This is where he came from."

"And that is the medical capsule," Odile said.

<We've reached the current moment,> Ven informed Lucan as Myr said, "So how do we—"

A ghost dropped into the clearing from above. A Jijikine in a pale, ribbon-wrapped cincorro battlesuit lowered noiselessly from the stasis hull. Powder swirled around her. The other two members of Jijikine glided forward, inhumanly graceful except for the jerky motions of their HAWs, targeting first one homesteader then another, using an old strategy to keep a crowd frightened.

Except homesteaders didn't scare that easy.

"We're unarmed, scrubjack," Elishiva told Jijikine. "We came to speak with you."

Low-resolution features flickered onto the nearest cincorro faceplate. "You came at the risk of further contamination."

Odile growled, "Life *is* contamination. Unlike massacring the innocent, which is—"

The Jijikine swiped at Odile, slashing a bloody curve along their arm with an extruded forearm-blade.

Blood welled between Odile's fingers when they grabbed the wound, and Lucan tensed in the shadows and asked, <You done getting our records?>

<I haven't started.>

<What the tzek? Are you connected?>

<Yes, but I'm still—> The pause was almost imperceptible as Ven reduced the complexity of her concepts to his level. <—reinforcing the correlation between myself and my host to ensure—>

<How long do you need?>

<Not more than a hundred seconds,> she said.

He felt her withholding information. <What aren't you telling me?>

<Later,> she said.

"Speak," Jijikine told Elishiva, in that pleasant synthetic voice.

"We came—" Elishiva exhaled when a HAW pointed at her face. "We were following a beacon to your base when we—"

"Why?"

"To ask that you release Lucan."

"Why?"

Elishiva pulled her oxygen veil down, revealing her face. "Because life is precious."

"Continue," Jijikine said.

"We spotted you coming this way." Elishiva paused. "There's no reason to take irreversible action. Let's discuss this without weapons, without violence, like—"

"Like you didn't with Saadya." Izzy scowled at the nearest battlesuit. "You murdering meltholes, I hope you—"

A HAW stock smashed her in the stomach, doubling her over. The Jijikine battered her to the ground and she whimpered and crawled away from the blows— toward the medical chamber, toward Lucan's hiding space.

He narrowed his arcpistol beam to a pinprick that still couldn't penetrate the armor and—

A Velikor fired from the shadows, a quick burst that caught the Jijikine in the side of the head.

<Hester,> Ven explained. Unnecessarily, for once.

The rounds flattened against coalescing cincorro fibers, then tumbled into the powdery haze covering the ground. The Jijikine spun unhurriedly—unhurt—and returned fire. A laser pulse vanished across the crash site, and Ven flicked Lucan a single image: of Hester, braced in a stateroom doorway as the roof collapsed onto her.

The hum of a laser-activated HAW changed pitch. The featureless Jijikine switched output like she had before massacring the mossback's family

Elishiva said, "Wait! We want to talk to your commander."

"That is no longer possible," Jijikine told her.

"Listen. Listen to me. There's no reason for anyone else to get hurt."

"That, too, is no longer possible."

Still clenching their wounded arm, Odile stepped forward. "We're not going to fight you."

"That is acceptable," the delicate-faced Jijikine said, and the featureless one opened fire.

Odile's leg ruptured at the knee, and Myr exploded in a blast of blood and viscera. On the ground, Izzy screamed.

The laser pulse was sweeping toward the rest of the home-steaders when Ven's solution bloomed in Lucan's mind.

• • •

<Are you sure?> he asked her.
　<Yes.>
　<The price is—>
　<—one we're willing to pay. Gehenna, hon, you're *eager*.>
　<Since when do we listen to me?>
　<I don't know if there are things we won't do anymore,> Ven told him. <But there are things we won't accept.>

• • •

Ven triggered the medical capsule's self-destruct mechanism.
　There was a hollow *whoomp* and Jijikine spun toward the noise an instant before the shock wave flooded through the open airlock. The blast wasn't strong enough to damage anyone: just enough to blow a billion dead nanoparticles into the air.
　The dust reduced visibility to a few centimeters, blinding the cincorro sensors—but Ven filtered Lucan's senses and he advanced fast into the clearing. His useless sidearm was in his left hand, so he ducked toward Izzy and snatched her k-stick with his right.
　Crouching and pivoting, he fired three times through the haze. Not trying to hit Jijikine, just keeping them focused on him instead of the homesteaders. Except despite how he'd angled his shots, one of them backtraced the trajec-

tories with terrifying accuracy, scorching a tunnel through the dust a centimeter from his nose.

His adrenaline spiked, and Ven channeled the energy into a dive and a roll.

"Oh, shit, oh, no," Izzy gasped. "You murdered her, you fucking meltholes killed Myr."

"You're in shock, Odile," Elishiva said, her voice strong. "I'm applying a tourniquet, eyes open, look at me my love, you're in shock."

Lucan surged to his feet behind the delicate-faced Jijikine and fired twice at the featureless one, who immediately returned an incandescent fusillade.

The blasts scorched the delicate one's battlesuit. Nothing penetrated, though, and the attack stopped when Jijikine realized she was firing on her own team.

The delicate one turned toward Lucan … exactly as Ven anticipated. She'd already started Lucan spinning along with the Jijikine, moving in a twirling dance while the k-stick eased between bands of the battlesuit at the armpit.

Cincorros were impervious to long-range, high-energy attacks, they he had to do this the old-fashioned way: Lucan grunted and slammed the blade toward the man's axillary artery.

The razor edge sliced through underlayer and muscle and into the nerve cluster.

The Jijikine shrieked and his suit squealed, notifying his squad of his critical status. As he dropped, Lucan crouched in place, because Ven projected that the remaining Jijikines would assume he was moving.

Maybe they did, maybe they didn't, but they held fire. Either they couldn't target through the dust or they were afraid of hitting their injured squad-mate. The stab had disabled his cincorro. Finally, a lucky break.

<That's not luck, that's suit depletion. Running analysis on—> Ven fell silent when the scarified Jijikine loomed at them through the dust.

She'd retracted a strip of the cincorro armor across her face to nullify the dust's effect on her sensors. She was tracking Lucan with her naked eyes. She was stronger and faster than he was, but she didn't have Ven sharpening her senses so she advanced too close and couldn't bring her HAW to bear.

She compensated by stabbing at him with a wrist-blade.

He blocked with the barrel of his sidearm and fired at her ribs from five centimeters away, which didn't do anything except leave a smudge.

Shit.

The Jijikine followed through with a flurry of blows. Lucan blocked with the k-stick and arcpistol. After a brief, rhythmic clacking, she brushed aside his defenses. Her elbow whipped at his face and her blade slashed at his stomach. She was trying to break his neck and disembowel him in the same motion, and he couldn't dodge both.

Ven made the choice.

He hunched to take the elbow on the dome of his head and Ven handled the pain while the blade carved an incision in his side. He shoved his pistol forward, nosing the muzzle between the bands of the cincorro battlesuit, and fired once before another blow knocked him backward.

The Jijikine shrugged her HAW into position. She stutter-stepped forward, keeping him in sight. Her barrel swept closer to a killshot and he was too slow to dodge, too hurt to attack. He couldn't stop this; he couldn't save them.

She started engaging the trigger and—

• • •

<Perhaps I *should* tell you now,> Ven said, stopping time to update him about the information she'd been withholding.

<Because 'later' is looking unlikely?>

<Because you should know who you are.>

<I thought you didn't get our records. I thought we just blew them up.>

<I didn't, and we did. However, that doesn't mean I learned nothing.>

The HAW was nine degrees from the center of Lucan's chest. A motionless puff of dust sheathed the barrel.

Ven said, <Adjunct Teom Lucan. XC-541A. You fought in the war.>

<The war's been over for eighty years.>

<Closer to ninety.>

<Wait. I fought in the *war?*> The HAW remained fixed in place, the motes of dust hung motionless, but everything changed. <Because ... because that isn't a medical capsule, it's a stasis capsule.>

<Yes. A reparative stasis chamber. Which roused us when you regained minimal functionality after decades of treatment. That is what caught everyone's attention.>

His mind reeled in the unmoving world. <You're saying, you're telling me we were in there for *eighty years?*>

<Closer to ninety.>

<How? Why?>

<Station constructed five heedships to end the war. Each was captained by a human mind uploaded into a command matrix. Each was paired with an adjunct.>

He said, <You're a ship. You became a ship.>

<I'm a ship.>

<You crashed when the fleets dropped from the sky.>

<Yes.>

<*That's* your host? The matrix where your mind uploaded is a battleship?>

A wordless affirmative. <I believe that I ejected you and this local, limited version of myself directly into the Marigold. I believe that I curtailed our memory to give us an opportunity to start again, in the future. To start anew.>

<So I was right all along! About forgetting the past and making new lives here.>

Ven laughed in surprise. <*That* is your takeaway?>

<Let me have my little victories.> He considered for a timeless moment. <Who were you before you became a ship? Who was I? And what's your official designation? The Vengeance? The Venerable? The Vendetta.>

<I've no idea. We just blew up the records, Lucan, in the medical capsule. I pieced this together from tenuous scraps.>

<So you're a heedship and I'm a hundred years old.>

<Yes.>

<You survived the crash—I mean, the *other* you. The ship-you. You crashed somewhere, but you're damaged. You don't know your own location and now, once Jijikine pulls the trigger, we'll never find you.>

<On the bright side, you *were* right all along,> she told him.

<I was?>

<You and me, we're not new to each other. We're a bonded pair.>

<Joined at the root,> he said, and neither of them could think of better last words than those.

• • •

The HAW barrel was two degrees from the center of Lucan's chest. When Ven released the flow of time, the Jijikine engaged the trigger—but jerked wildly before firing.

The wild jerk threw off her aim.

The wild jerk was Izzy, on the ground, yanking at Jijikine's ankle.

The HAW barrel
swung
down,
a handspan from Izzy's terrified,
stubborn, grooved face
and fired once.

Then Lucan was staggering, off-balance and crumpling. He landed on a spike of pain and started rolling. The homesteaders were shouting; Izzy was dead. The fallen, bleeding Jijikine was groaning—in his own voice instead of the synthetic one—and a concussion was spreading across Lucan's brain.

His vision doubled and blurred. He was woozy and weak, two seconds from losing consciousness …

Ven seized control. She pushed him to his knees, and he braced to meet the scarified Jijikine's next attack. He didn't see her, though, despite the air that was clearing too fast around him—because she was down.

She was dead, splattered all over the inside of her battlesuit.

Apparently if he gently infiltrated his arcpistol muzzle through the layered armor before firing, there was no defense. She'd taken a blast to her bare skin. Her suit kept her functional for a few second but she was dead now and darkness frayed his vision—

<One more, hon,> Ven said, injecting him with a cocktail of stimulants and painkillers.

His vision snapped into focus. One more.

The haze thinned to shoulder-level and condensed below that. He crawled away from the Jijikine he's shot, across the murky clearing toward the one he'd stabbed, who was twitching and moaning and dying. Ven fed him flashes of the third battlesuit. An exposed band of armor revealed her dark enraged eyes inside that featureless helmet. She was crouching, trying to find a shot, spinning like a g-dancer as the dust cloud settled down to her chest, then waist.

Lucan stayed lower—and started to laugh. Too many drugs, too many revelations. The sound was unhinged and Jijikine's HAW rattled across the clearing. Slugs thunked into bulkheads and floor-panels.

The dust settled to knee height as the remaining Jijikine swept for Lucan.

She couldn't detect a trace of him, not a shadow. As the air cleared, the airlock reappeared across the clearing. Next came the silhouette of nanocryonic regulators. Then the top half of the stabbed Jijikine, who was supine on a dust-hidden mound of rubble. Only his chest-plate and blank helmet appeared above the particulate fog.

He was twitching faintly, and a hoarse groan of agony sounded.

"Rendering assistance," the other Jijikine said, after a final sweep.

Her synthetic voice was so affectless that Lucan almost wondered if she was human. But when she trotted toward her fallen comrade, her eyes, revealed by the retracted strip of battlesuit, were burning with anger.

Good.

She knelt beside the injured Jijikine and addressed the homesteaders in that pleasant voice: "If he survives, I will kill you before departing. If he dies, I will proceed to your valley and kill every—"

Lucan punched upward from beneath the delicate-faced Jijikine, extending the k-stick through the woman's eye.

She crumpled to the ground centimeters away. The delicate Jijikine—the one he'd stabbed first—was a crushing weight on Lucan's chest. Not injured anymore: dead. Lucan had wormed beneath him under the cover of the dust, his movements hidden by the man's dying twitches.

Those moans of agony had been genuine, though. Lucan knew that, because he'd been the one moaning. Another moan sounded, a weaker one …

Ven said, <Shhh. Sleep, honey. Sleep. I've got you.>

21

<The planet is called Elam, though the official designation is 'The River Is a Mirror That Flows Through All Our Hearts, KHT 3382 Elam-b' and—>

<We've already been through this,> Lucan said.

<You're effectively unconscious again,> Ven told him.

<And that's your way of telling me? By repeating planetary data? Wait! Is this another joke?>

She refused to answer. <We are in the crawler again.>

<With Hester? She survived?>

<Yes. She's the only one who can drive this thing.>

<She shot me in the back.>

<Are you ready for a briefing?>

<I'm ready for a little R&R.>

Ven raised a briefing flag. <We accomplished three mission objectives.>

<I can think of one: we know who we are now. At least, in general. You're an antique heedship, I'm your antique crew. Still no specifics?>

<No, and I'm not sure we'll find any outside of my primary location.>

<You mean, the databanks of your crashed ship. Your lost body.>

<Yes.>

<Huh. If I'm not a scrubjack, why is this mark on my face?>

<The Servants adopt terminology from previously existing military units: Tribune, Oficira, and so forth. They also adopt insignia, like that on your face.>

<Ah.>

<Second, my connection to my host is firmly established now, though extremely limited.>

<So she's not trapped inside her own hull anymore?>

<She's still trapped, but not in deprivation. Not in solitary confinement. She's not alone anymore.> Ven shared an upwelling of joyous reprieve. <However, we cannot communicate. The data flows in one direction only: from us to her. And it is comprised almost entirely of sensory information.>

<So she's locked inside her hull, but we're her eyes on the outside world?>

<Near enough. She—I—can survive much longer now. Without fragmenting, without decompensating.>

<As long as we keep showing her the sights?>

<That's the good news.>

<Which implies you're about to tell me the 'even better' news.>

<Establishing the connection exhausted my resources. I didn't locate her.>

<So we've got to find another crash site? On a planet with thousands? And we don't have any clue where to start?>

<We have one clue,> Ven said.

<Yeah? What'd you find?>

Amusement bubbled through her. <Nothing. You're the one who found it.>

<Me? When?>

<I discovered it in your memory while you recovered. Our third mission achievement.>

She replayed his experience of being connected to her host. How he'd shrunk to an ant on a craggy mountainside. Tiny and uncomprehending as an enormous shape rose around him, a jagged monolith …

He said, <The mountain! It's a real place. I didn't just imagine it.>

<My host transferred that image to you. It's the last recording before her sensors failed.>

<Your ship is *there*. Your host is there. That mountain.>

<I believe so.>

<When we find the mountain, we find *you*.>

<Yes.>

<So we'll check the Grandmothers' geological surveys. I'll ask Elishiva for maps when we get back.>

<It's not that simple,> she said.

<What does that mean?>

Instead of answering, Ven roused him in the crawler.

He wasn't cuffed in the passageway this time. He wasn't even tucked into one of the coffin-sized compartments. He was on a makeshift bunk in the cockpit, nestled beneath an ornate blanket as Hester drove across the wasteland, busily adjusting the controls. Oh, no; she was busily *embroidering* while monitoring the autopilot.

Lucan was wearing a medical gown, which made sense, but Bonavent's weapon was unsecured in a holster beside him, which didn't. So what he did was, he checked the arcpistol. Charged and ready, and comforting in his fist.

"In case you want to shoot me," Hester said, without turning around.

"Tempting," he said, but he wasn't angry at her betrayal. Though he didn't know why. <Are you blanking my emotions?>

<No. You're not angry because you would've done the same in her position, to protect the people you love.>

<Oh, bullshit. >

Ven did the internal equivalent of rolling her eyes, and he returned the pistol to the holster.

Hester said, over the sound of her embroidery thimbles, "If you're tired of nutritional infusion, there's real food in the drawer."

Lucan pushed himself into a seated position and felt surprisingly okay. He grabbed a crunchy bun and a fermented drink then took the seat beside Hester.

The goldenrod sky was intense over rolling hills and gentle gullies. Lightning danced around a mesa dominating the landscape. Ven drank in the stark beauty like—like lifegiving nutritional infusion—but Lucan preferred the lush oasis of the valley. That was his idea of R&R: a few days in bed, sleeping and eating and sleeping. Then a few days outside, helping homesteaders with the chores, learning how to live again.

"How far is the valley?" he asked.

"Two days," Hester said.

"Two *days*?"

"Behind us." When she turned toward him, she was wearing an eyepatch. Embroidered, of course. "And we're heading the other direction."

<You were keeping this a secret?> he asked.

<I'm letting Hester tell you.>

"What happened?" he asked.

"Jijikine dropped a roof on me." Hester sighed in mock-tragedy. "I'm not as beautiful as I once was."

"That's okay, you've still got a terrible personality. Where are we headed?"

"Into the great unknown." A gentle smile rose on her face. "After you handled the scrubjacks, Elishiva dragged us to the valley for medical treatment."

"I've been unconscious that long?"

"Four days in a self-induced medical coma, running some internal recovery process that nobody's seen before."

<Nanotech medical device,> Ven prompted.

"Nanotech trauma shit," he said.

"And where you get your hands on that?" Hester asked.

"All I know is, it doesn't heal amnesia."

She shot him an amused, dubious look. "That's your warware?"

"Mm. So what happened?"

"I recovered first. Well, to the extent you see before you—homesteader medics don't stock prosthetic eyes. And ..." Her amusement faded. "Elishiva told me that I'm not welcome there anymore."

"In the valley?"

"Yes. She asked me to leave."

"Why?"

"Because I shot you in the back and gave you to the scrubjacks."

Great. He was finally pissed, but he was pissed *for* Hester instead of *at* her. "What were you supposed to do? That was your only play."

"I told her you'd say that, and she said, 'We would take Lucan's opinion into account if it wasn't worthless.'"

"So she'll face down cincorro battlesuits to save my ass, but doesn't care what I think?"

"Homesteaders and faith, what can I tell you?" Hester gestured at her controls, magnifying a portion of desert on her screen. "I hear you tore through the containment squad pretty definitively."

"I guess."

"Homesteaders aren't big on brutality, Lucan."

"So I'm not welcome, either?"

"No, you got a pass this time. They don't think you know better."

"Then why am I here?"

Hester took the drink from his hand and sipped. "You're a danger to the valley. Another containment team will roll up sooner or later, gunning for you."

"Oh, so they sent me off with you. That makes sense."

"It makes extremely good sense. Except *they* didn't send you."

"Huh?"

"They wanted to keep you there. They didn't care about the risk." Her opalescent eye glimmered. "So I stole you away in the middle of the night."

He snorted a laugh. "You kidnapped me!"

"Goodness, no. You're free to leave."

"You just temporarily relocated me?"

"Exactly." Hester gesture-guided the crawler around a patch of tufted lichen. "So where do you want to go? Hargisa City? A reef town? Maybe the slot canyons."

"Anywhere I want, huh?"

"Just say the word."

Lucan gazed at the viewscreen, letting the stark beauty of the alien world wash through him. Through him and Ven, and into her host.

First they'd find this mountain. They'd locate Ven's crashed ship, and reunite the broken parts of her fractured self. And after that? After that, they'd find a cottage, in a meadow, with a view of the sky.

ACKNOWLEDGEMENTS

Many thanks to Ian Mallett, Caitlin Blasdell, and the team at Realm who worked on the novella: Diana M. Pho, Alexis Latshaw, Kyndal Thomas, Mary Assadullahi, Tara Sonin and Heather Mason.

ABOUT THE AUTHOR

As the son of an Army private, an Air Force staff sergeant, and an elementary school teacher, Joel Dane was raised on war stories and inter-service rivalry—and a stubborn faith in humanity that explains the solarpunk elements in his books. He's the author of more than twenty novels, including the *Cry Pilot* military sci-fi trilogy. He wrote a dozen episodes of a Netflix Original Series, and the audio drama podcast *Marigold Breach*.

Visit him online at www.joeldane.com.

www.ingramcontent.com/pod-product-compliance
Lightning Source LLC
Chambersburg PA
CBHW031238260626
47169CB00007B/2364